THE SPEED MERCHANTS

72

The Speed Merchants

by WILL COOK

DUELL, SLOAN AND PEARCE

New York

First edition

Affiliate of
MEREDITH PRESS
Des Moines & New York

Library of Congress Catalogue Card Number: 64-24484

Manufactured in the United States of America for Meredith Press

VAN REES PRESS   •   NEW YORK

To JESSIE ALFORD NUNN
friend and educator

CONTENTS

THE SPEED MERCHANTS

Chapter 1

A NEW JOB

At the intersection, Skip Hudson brought his Austin Healey to a stop, checked for traffic, and then swung onto Willow Pass Road, chirping the rear tires a little when he shifted. Cruising at a steady sixty, he let the California wind buffet him and blow through his close-cropped hair. He drove for a mile, leaving behind the used-car lots and the drive-in hamburger places. As he entered a section of furniture stores and plumbing shops, he reduced his speed and then down-shifted before he turned into Jim Vale's Automotive and parked in the area reserved for customers.

Skip was early; he had intended to be, and he checked his face in the rear-view mirror to make sure his shave had caught everything. His hair was a light brown, faded by the constant summer sun. His skin was tanned golden, and a scatter of freckles peppered the bridge of his nose and forehead.

He got out of the car and looked at the shop. It was a huge complex of three buildings built into a large U, with

3

the office surrounded by green grass and a carefully mani-
cured flower garden.

A bright yellow bus came down the highway, tires
humming; it slowed and turned in, going around the building to park in back. A few minutes later a stocky man
came through the office, opened the front door, and walked
down the wide stone sidewalk.

He was a big man with a wrestler's shoulders and a face
that looked as though it had once or twice made a sudden
stop against an unyielding object. He looked at Skip Hudson, and then said, "Which one are you?"

"Hudson."

The man looked at the empty parking lot. "Where are
the others?"

"I don't know," Skip said frankly. He glanced at his
watch. "Your secretary said eight o'clock. It's five to. Are
you Mr. Vale?"

The man nodded. "Come on in," he said.

Hudson followed him into the building. The showroom was crowded with engines on stands, magnesium
racing wheels, and bins crammed with special racing parts.
Straight ahead was the parts counter, sixty feet long. To
the left of the foyer lay a cluster of offices, like glassed
cribs; Skip and Vale went that way, through one office to
Vale's private retreat.

There was a thick rug on the floor, along with massive
furniture, and pictures of racing cars and drivers on the
walls. Vale motioned the boy to sit down.

Vale leaned back in his chair and looked steadily at
Skip. "First job?"

"No, sir. Right now I'm working at the Volkswagen

place," Skip said. "Before that I bagged groceries at Safe-way."

Vale lit a cigarette and blew smoke toward the ceiling. "What do you do at Volkswagen?"

"I started on the lube rack six months ago. Now I'm doing some mechanical work."

"And now you want to work for me," Vale said. "I've got a big business going here. A new car showroom on River Street, a big used-car lot farther down Willow Pass, and the plant here. I need a man in the shop. What makes you think you'll qualify?"

He was, Skip decided, like some fellow who sat next to you at a ball game and kept gouging you in the ribs, only Vale did it with words, short, hard counterpunches.

"I'm a pretty good mechanic," Skip said, "and I'm not stupid. I think I can learn anything your men can teach me."

This frankness surprised Vale, and then he laughed and knocked the ash off his cigarette. "I have three departments here. One is general service and parts. Another is engine rebuilding, and the third is the competition department. I race cars, and many of my customers race their cars, and I maintain this department to service them. The quality of the work is very exact. The man I want will start at the bottom and work up. If he doesn't show me anything, he goes out the door. I don't want a kid who's here today and gone tomorrow. I want loyalty to me and to the firm." He butted out his cigarette. "Is that your car outside?"

"Yes, sir."

"Mind if I take a look at it?" He was already getting up, as though an objection wouldn't matter anyway. They went out together, and Jim Vale walked around the Austin Healey several times. Then he said, "There's something familiar about this car. Not many of these four-banger LeMans Healeys around. Mind telling me where you got it?"

"From a wrecking yard. I bought it two years ago. Someone had raced it and wiped it out and—"

"Sure!" Vale said, snapping his fingers. "Les Malloy's car! He went end for end at Torrey Pines. Who did the body work for you?"

"I did. All of it."

Vale looked at him skeptically. "Where did you learn body work? In school?"

"Some in auto shop. My stepfather is the body man at Volkswagen."

Jim Vale laughed. "So that's how you got your job there. Pull."

That stung Skip's temper, but he held it. "I had the job before he knew anything about it."

A chopped Chevrolet came in with a squeal of tires; two boys got out and came over, looking at the Austin Healey. "What'll it do in the quarter?" one asked.

"I don't drag it," Skip said.

"'Fraid you'll break it?" He was a toothy boy, always grinning.

"Let's just say that I have a thousand dollars in it that I don't want to lose," Skip said.

The boy rolled his eyes and hitched up his unbelted jeans, and the other one stood there cuffing the blacktop with his toe. A raked pickup came in, and before the driver shut it off he revved the engine, making the tail pipes snore loudly. The young man got out, came over to Jim Vale, and said, "You the boss?" He grinned and looked at Hudson. "Hi, Skip."

"Hi, Larry," Skip said. He remembered the young man because there had been a fuss over his last year at school. Larry had been graduated but hadn't attended the ceremony; all the graduates had talked about it.

"You wait here," Vale said and motioned for Skip to follow him back inside. He dropped two dimes into the Coke machine and gave one to Skip. "Go on back to the shop and look around. The competition department is straight back. Don't fiddle with things. I'll talk to these clowns."

"I'll keep my hands in my pockets," Skip said and went on back.

The shop area was large, and the machine shop had a cyclone fence around it and a stout lock on the sliding gate. There were Lotus and Cooper racing cars in the bays, some stripped of all body work, some partially disassembled.

The engine department was glass-enclosed, and the interior was white, and hospital clean. There were no tools cluttered about, no grease spots on the painted floor, and only the hum of the air conditioner in some other part of the building broke the silence.

Skip could hear a large electric clock whirring on the south wall, marking off the time, and he suddenly felt very lonely. This was not a new feeling for him; he had known it off and on all his life and he often wondered if it would ever go away.

This ache was connected with his father, whom Skip

could remember occasionally as a laughing, pipe-smoking man, always squeezing his son hard when he picked him up. Then the image would go away and there would be no memory at all. Skip felt guilty about that, as though he had failed his father.

It had never seemed fair to Skip that a man who had fought in one war should be made to fight in another five years later, but it had been that way, and he supposed it was that way with others. Korea was a long way from California, and after the telegram came their life was very different. His mother sold the house and got a smaller place. She banked the insurance and looked for a job, something that didn't keep her away from home too much.

And it didn't really matter how hard she tried, because there were things the boy had to learn to do for himself. He learned early that money was not easy to come by; he mowed lawns and bicycled around a paper route and then watched his earnings disappear into the impersonal maw of the bank. There was only a small gray book with steadily mounting figures to show for his labor.

He couldn't remember when he began to wonder if his mother would ever get married again; he supposed it was in his twelfth or thirteenth year. It was just something he had never thought about, but suddenly he wondered if his mother ever did. She had never showed an interest in men.

Then Otto Hansen bought the house next door. He was from Germany, a newly naturalized citizen, and he spoke with hardly an accent at all. Skip mowed his lawn and trimmed his hedge and Otto twice got their ancient forty-nine Chevrolet running when old age began to make it balky.

It seemed strange now that love had bloomed under his nose without his becoming aware of it, but it had. Otto was a good man, very tall and slender, in his early forties, and rather grave most of the time. His wife had been killed in the bombings of Hamburg, and he had first gone to Canada to work after the war. There wasn't much doubt that he was the best body man in town and had more work than he could handle.

Skip often stopped at Otto's place and watched him work, then walked home with him in the evening. It gave him a good feeling he couldn't explain, and he didn't try, half afraid that if he did the feeling would go away.

Then one night, just as it was getting dark, he came home from a ball game and his mother met him at the kitchen door. Otto was in the parlor and wanted to talk to him.

He had on his good suit and his manner was more grave than usual. Skip remembered it all clearly, the man's sincere manner, his genuine concern; he wanted to marry Skip's mother but would not do so if Skip held a real objection.

Skip supposed that this was the way things were done in Europe, but then getting married was a pretty solemn thing. The picture of his father, taken on his wedding day, showed a solemn man, one who could smile but didn't feel like it then.

So after seven years of fatherless life, Skip got Otto Hansen. Nothing was quite the same after that. His mother quit her work because Otto wouldn't have it any other way. She laughed a lot and Otto played the accordion very well, and knew a limitless number of songs, which he sang in a better than average voice. They got a dog that they called Fritz, and Fritz howled when Otto sang. Otto whistled when he went to work and he was whistling when he came home.

Still some things remained the same. Otto was a man of thrift. He wasn't tight with his money, but careful with it, and he believed that a boy should have work to do, chores around the house, and a part-time job to help take care of his future.

A door opened and Jim Vale came back into the shop, breaking into Skip Hudson's thoughts. "How do you like the place?" Vale asked, and then went on before Skip offered an opinion. "I started in 1946 with three thousand dollars and a boat load of English cars. Anglias and Hillmans in those days, with a few MGs, when I could get 'em." He chuckled. "No one but a nut bought those cars then, but I sold 'em, and sometimes I promised that they'd run forever to do it." He waved his arm to include it all. "Vale Automotive, owned by one man and run by one man, and if you remember that, you'll have this job a long time."

"Does that mean you're going to hire me?" Skip asked.

Vale grinned. "I thought you were a bright boy." He handed him three sheets of paper. "These are rules. We live by 'em around here. Know 'em by tomorrow. Break any of 'em and you draw your time right then. We open this place at nine and close at five. The mechanics get here at eight forty-five and leave at five thirty. The competition department puts in a lot of overtime and weekends. Any man who works for me gets paid for what he does, as long as he does something to get paid for." He shook out a cigarette and lit it. "You might as well understand right away that I've got some pet dislikes. One of 'em is German cars. So forget what you learned at Volkswagen and I'll forget you ever worked there."

Skip Hudson felt slightly battered by the man's forthright manner, yet he plunged on and asked, "Maybe I ought to know what the others are, Mr. Vale."

The big man stared for a moment, then shrugged. "You want it straight, I'll give it to you straight. I particularly dislike your stepfather, Otto Hansen. Six years ago I offered him a deal no sane man could have resisted. He could have made a pile of money, but he turned me down. He was pretty blunt about it too."

"Otto says what he thinks," Skip agreed.

"Start in the morning," Vale said, cutting off the conversation.

He went back to his office and Skip followed a short distance behind; Vale had his office door closed when Skip went out.

The office staff had arrived and were leaving their cars; Skip stepped to one side of the walk to let them by. Other cars were pulling around to the rear of the building and were parked there, Skip supposed that these were the mechanics. He noticed that the raked pickup truck was still sitting there and then a three-year-old Jaguar coupe turned in, started past, and stopped with a sudden setting of the brakes.

A tall, blond man got out and came over as Skip was slipping into the bucket seat. The man looked at the car very carefully, and then said, "Excuse me, old boy, but could you tell me where you got this car?"

"Pacific Wrecking. Why?"

The man was circling the car, smiling. "I'm Les Malloy, and I do believe this was once mine." He patted the aluminum hood. "It was a bit crumpled when I last saw it." A car pulled in and because Malloy's Jaguar was blocking the way, the driver honked. Malloy hurriedly got in, calling, "Drop around and see me! I'm shop foreman!" And then he drove off around the building. Skip put the key in his ignition, but before he could start up his car, the young man in the pickup jumped out and came over. "You got the job, huh?" He bumped the side of the car with his knee. "Watch where you park this thing, huh flake?"

Then he dashed for his pickup and snarled away, tires screaming. Skip watched him go, then started the Healey. He backed around and a young girl ran out, looking both ways. Then she saw him and her alarm vanished.

"I thought someone had an accident," she said. She looked about a year younger than he; her hair and eyes were dark and a nice figure filled out a print dress.

"Just some jerk starved for attention," he said. "You work here?"

"File clerk in parts." She made walking motions with her fingers. "It makes for nimble fingers and weak eyes, going through all those cards."

"I start tomorrow," Skip said and introduced himself. "Do you go to Ridgeway High?"

"Canfield."

"Then what?"

"Suppose I tell you during lunch hour tomorrow. Mr. Vale has fits when he catches someone loafing on company time."

"What's your name?"

"Anne Bechel."

She hurried inside, and he backed out and headed for the center of town. Willow Pass led straight into Third Street; he had to wait for the light to change, then he turned and went down two blocks before cutting over to First.

The Volkswagen dealer occupied a large building on a corner lot. Skip parked in the street near his stepfather's place. Otto Hansen had the doors of his paint booth closed and the compressor was going at full speed, so Skip went through the service entrance to the shop foreman's office.

Charlie Manly was adding up a customer's bill; he finished it and put it on a stack for the accounting department. He lit a smoke and said, "How did you make out with Vale?"

"He hired me," Skip said. "It sure wasn't like getting in here, Mr. Manly."

"No, I could have told you that. You'll find a lot of things different at Vale's. And it's more than working on two makes of cars." He sighed and smiled. "I ought to let you learn this yourself. But I'm going to tell you something to remember: Jim Vale never gave anything away in his life that he didn't get back double for it. So watch him when he starts handing out the things that look free."

"I don't quite know what you mean," Skip said.

"Just remember it, and you'll soon know," Manly said. He grinned. "Now clear out of here. I can't have former employees hanging around my office." Then when Skip opened the door, Manly said, "You come back and see me now and then, you hear?"

Chapter 2

SKIP MEETS THE PROS

Otto hansen was still in the booth when Skip left, so he drove home, cut the grass, raked and burned the clippings, and then got in his car and went back to his stepfather's body shop. Hansen was cleaning up; he put everything away each night and swept out the place. Skip helped him, and then Otto locked up and got into Skip's car.

"I feel like a cup of coffee," Otto said. He laughed. "I'll buy."

"Now how can I turn that down?" Skip said, and drove four blocks over to a small drive-in restaurant. They went inside and sat in a booth, where the waitress brought them coffee.

Hansen remained silent for a time. Then he said, "It would have been nice if you'd gone on to college, Skip."

"I don't think it's for me, Otto." The boy smiled. "You know I never carried better than a C in high school. I'm just not the book type, that's all."

"You got straight A's in German two years in a row."

"Because I had you for a teacher," Skip said. "Otto, you made it exciting for me. It was a real challenge."

"And now you'll work for Jim Vale. There's a challenge for you. To keep your feet on the ground while he's pulling your head in the clouds."

Skip's expression turned grave. "Otto, I think I can handle this."

"You're probably right," Otto Hansen said. "I think you are smart enough about people not to be fooled for long. Besides, we must be honest about this. Vale has the best place in four hundred miles. You can learn a lot there." He finished his coffee and slid out of the booth. "I've got the yard to mow before dark."

"Already mowed it," Skip said and winked. "I thought maybe we could get some work done on the boat. Unless you want to watch television."

"*Ach!*" Otto said. They went out and got into the Austin Healey.

They lived on West Allen Street, a broad avenue flanked by thick maple trees. The house, when Skip's mother bought it, had been small, but Otto Hansen had added onto it, built a patio, and gradually transformed it into one of the nicest homes on the street.

That Otto, Skip thought as he drove along, shooting a sidelong glance at his stepfather. There was a man who never seemed to waste a minute, a man who could work on five projects at a time and never fail to finish any of them.

Skip pulled into the driveway and parked alongside the family VW. His mother came out, a slender woman with light hair. She wore glasses, which kept slipping, and she kept pushing them back.

She kissed Otto, then Skip, and said, "Roast beef tonight. Twenty minutes. So don't putter and get your clothes dirty."

Skip said, "I got the job, Ma."

"Well, I'm glad and yet I'm not. That's a very attractive place for a young man. I think you could even call it glamorous. First thing you'll be doing is running up a bill."

"He knows better than that," Otto Hansen said.

"Yes, but we often do things when we know better," she said. "Vale's has been a dead end for more than a few promising young men. The Cady boy was all set for college, but he stayed on. Now he's Vale's parts manager. And that's a long way from—"

"From what?" Otto asked. "We don't know what he could have been, Ellen. Maybe that's all there was in the boy. I'm a body man. That's all that's in me."

"Otto, don't be a fool," she said and went into the house.

The rear lot was large and in one corner they had built a long shed with open sides to shelter the framed and planked hull of their sailboat. Skip and Otto had put in two years of spare-time work and had another two to go before they could have her hauled to the bay and lowered into the water. It had always been a dream of Otto Hansen to build a boat, and being a man highly skilled with tools, the project was coming along nicely, each step carefully thought out and executed.

They stood together, looking at the boat. After a

moment Skip said, "Otto, why did you turn Vale down when he offered you a job?"

"He told you that?" The man laughed softly. "Vale goes through life offering shiny things to people, knowing that there will always be people to accept them. But the shine never quite covers up the defects, Skip. I will work for a man, any man, but I won't sell myself to a man." He held out his hands. "These I sell. Not my mind or my heart. I insist on the right to think what I want."

"How can Jim Vale take that away?" Skip asked.

"You'll have to work for him and find out," Otto said. "Now let's not keep your mother waiting for supper."

By the time Skip Hudson had worked ten days for Vale Automotive, he understood that every department was operated at a profit, or at least reflected a profit in the over-all picture. The racing department was in this category, and Les Malloy was the foreman. His authority extended to the maintenance of the privately owned racing cars, and the cars raced as part of the Vale team.

This was expensive, but winning meant newspaper space, free advertising of the superiority of the Lotus cars, which sold cars and induced other racing drivers to switch to them.

Malloy was British, a tall man who always wore corduroy coats and his hair rather long. He spoke softly and smoked a pipe. There was nothing that went on in his department that he was not fully aware of, and often he supervised each phase, for racing car preparation was a meticulous thing, all hand work, careful machining, and precise fitting.

A Cortina-Ford engine, properly set up, was worth five thousand dollars, and the mechanics were not permitted to make any mistakes. Les Malloy saw to that. And he saw that Skip Hudson was, in time, going to make a good man. Malloy kept him busy as a helper, teaching him methods of assembly that would minimize chances of error. He soon had Skip working on different cars, packing experience into a small space of time; a man was only genuinely valuable when his training covered everything from suspension and body work to engine rebuilding.

And, as Malloy reported to Vale, another two years ought to turn the boy into a topflight racing mechanic.

Malloy made up the schedule for the mechanics who always went along with the cars for racing or testing. As he sat in his glassed-in office, trying to make up his mind, he saw Skip take the tail section off a Lotus 23 so he could fit a hydraulic throttle linkage. Malloy tapped his pencil against his teeth for a moment, and then put Skip Hudson's name down on the list for Saturday and Sunday.

It wasn't until quitting time, after Skip had washed and changed clothes, that he looked at the bulletin board and saw his name there, along with the rest of a crew. Malloy was still in his office and Skip knocked before stepping inside.

"I saw my name on the board, Mr. Malloy. What does that mean?"

"Just what it says. We're taking three cars for run-in and test at Fawndale on Saturday morning and remaining overnight. You can go, can't you?"

"Yes, sir!"

"So you know what it means," Malloy said and smiled

after Skip had left the office. He couldn't blame the young man for getting a little excited; he could remember his first trip to the circuit, when he'd worked hard and hoped that the car owners would come up and ask him if he'd like to take it around a few times. Finally one had done just that. A year later, Malloy found himself winning regularly, and he was signed up to drive the next season in Grand Prix cars. After eight years of that and some bad crashes, Malloy had simply given it up. His reputation had assured him employment in the automobile business and it had seemed profitable to come to America and sell those smart little British cars. Well, he'd done all that, made it and lost it to Jim Vale and now he worked for the man who'd taken it all. Malloy guessed that he'd go on working for Vale because there just wasn't anything else to do.

It might have been very different if he'd ever been the World Driving Champion, but of course he hadn't. He had been out there, winning now and then, but usually coming in third or fourth, a part of the big show, a handmaiden to drivers like Tony Brooks, Mike Hawthorne, Juan Fangio, and Stirling Moss. Malloy had been a good man but not a top man, and he supposed that was why he had lost to Jim Vale, who was a top man. That was Vale's place, on the summit, looking down on the rest of the world; Malloy could be quite philosophical about it now. Time had done that.

Skip Hudson was fifteen minutes early, yet by the time he parked his car and went around the building it was a quarter to eight. Les Malloy was waving directions to a mechanic who slowly eased the big diesel van up to the door, while another man pushed cars close to the down ramp.

A Lotus Elite came around the building, parked, and a rather small, wiry man got out and came over, limping slightly. Skip glanced at him. Something was vaguely familiar about him, but Skip couldn't put his finger on it until Malloy introduced them.

"Skip, this is Sandy Sanderson. Skip Hudson."

They shook hands and Skip looked into Sanderson's pale eyes with the wrinkles around them and nodded because he couldn't speak, not in front of this man who had won on just about every major racing circuit in Europe and America.

"I—I've got to help push the cars in the van," Skip said and hurried over to give the mechanics a hand. The Lotus racing cars were very light, the heaviest just weighing a thousand pounds; three men easily pushed them up the ramp and a hydraulic lift boosted the cars up so that four could be carried in the van at one time.

The two mechanics and Malloy rode in the van and Sanderson said, "Why don't you come along with me, Skip? No sense in driving your car too." They got into the Lotus Elite and Sanderson started the engine. He put his head out of the window and yelled at Malloy. "We'll go on ahead, Les!" He shifted into first and pulled out into the light traffic.

Fawndale racecourse lay eighteen miles to the east, a two and a quarter mile twister that had very few level spots in it. Sanderson drove around seventy. The Lotus loafed along and Skip Hudson held to a prolonged silence.

Finally Sanderson said, "You're sure a gabby one."

That made Skip laugh and he relaxed a little. "I just didn't know what to say, I guess."

"Going to drive a little?" Sanderson asked.

This surprised Skip. "Oh, no. I'll be running for beer and sandwiches for the crew."

"Don't kid yourself. These weekends are no lark. And if Vale ever found out one of his men opened a can of beer while on the job, he'd be drawing unemployment. This is my second year with Vale, and he makes no bones about the rules."

"I keep hearing that he's tough to work for," Skip said, "but so far I haven't even seen him in the shop."

"But he keeps track of you," Sanderson told him. "Jim Vale keeps close track of everything he owns."

"Just what does that mean?"

"A figure of speech, kid. Forget it."

"I wasn't trying to make you sore or anything," Skip said quickly.

"Sure, I know that. It's just that Vale gets under my skin once in awhile."

"If I didn't like a man," Skip said, "I'd quit."

"Sure, because you're young and it's all ahead of you. I'm thirty-two and if I quit Vale I'd make an enemy that would keep me out of race cars. And I can't afford that."

Sanderson pulled up to the contestant's gate, unlocked it, and drove along an access road to the pits, which were flanked by a solid row of cement buildings, built like a barracks. There was a carport shelter for the cars and a sleeping-dinette combination for mechanics who stayed overnight.

Near the start-finish line there was a larger building with Jim Vale's sign on it. Sanderson said, getting out of the car, "That's full of machine shop and parts. Here's the key." He tossed it to Skip, who opened the door and went inside. Sanderson came in and opened the roller overhead door so the van could unload right into the building. "We come here a lot with customers' cars, try them out, make suspension and rear-end ratio changes. That's why we keep all this equipment around here."

They could hear the diesel rig snorting through the gate and along the access road. A few minutes later it pulled up and backed to the garage door.

The cars were unloaded and the rear ends were jacked up before the engines were started. Over the rip of exhausts, Malloy outlined to Sanderson just what had to be done. The mechanics were adjusting the carburetors and Skip stood to one side, hands over his ears, trying to shut out the exhaust noise: keeeeeeeeooooooooobuuuuuuuu rrrrrrrriiiiiippppp; it was a continual rising and falling blast of sound and finally the mechanics were satisfied that the engines were putting out their power.

Malloy changed into a pair of driving coveralls. Sanderson simply put on a helmet and eased himself into the tiny car; he fastened his seat belt and shoulder harness and charged out of the pit area with tires smoking. He let the exhaust note build to a frightening rip, shifted very fast and kept on accelerating.

Malloy came out, got into his car, and charged after Sanderson. When he was well down the straight, one of the mechanics said, "They'll do a couple of laps and then have a go at it." He spoke to no one in particular; it was simply a statement of what he knew was to come.

Skip Hudson climbed onto the pit wall and one of the mechanics handed him a clipboard with a row of stop watches fastened to it. "Keep time, will you? They'll want to know their times when they come in."

Skip spent nearly an hour on the low wall, punching the watches when each came by, and then jotting down the times on the sheet. It soon became apparent to him that Malloy was not as fast as Sanderson, but he was more consistent; he continually turned laps within tenths of a second of each other, but Sanderson would often be off a second and a half.

And Malloy was edging up on Sanderson, a bit at a time, picking up a half a second here and there, for Sanderson never seemed to be able to quite regain the time he had lost. Finally they were circulating so close that they almost touched coming out of the last hairpin and onto the straightaway. After going around twice this way, Sanderson pulled into the pits, shut off, and loudly complained about not being able to get full power. The mechanics were clearing away the rear section when Les Malloy came in.

He claimed to be losing power.

The two mechanics poked their heads into the machinery; then one said something and pointed to a bracket on the fire wall. The aluminum had split, letting the throttle linkage develop slack so that the driver could not open the throttles.

"What the devil makes those things break?" Malloy

asked, almost to himself. "All right, better here than in a race. Put on a hydraulic throttle linkage."

"That Mickey Mouse," one of the mechanics said, but turned to the van to get the parts.

Sandy Sanderson was standing there, looking at the broken throttle linkage. He said, "They always develop cracks around the rivet holes, don't they?"

No one had asked Skip, but he had a suggestion. "Why don't you fasten the brackets on with epoxy resins?"

"Don't be funny," Malloy said.

"I wasn't. The hot rodders glue a lot of their machinery togeth—"

"This is not a hot rod," Malloy said, his manner snappy. "It's a nine-thousand-dollar car, built to exacting stand-ards, and any problems will be dealt with in a sound, well-engineered manner."

Sanderson, standing by Malloy, was shaking his head, advising Skip to quit talking, but the boy ignored him. "I didn't mean to make you sore, Mr. Mal—"

"Well, you are!" Malloy barked.

Sanderson stepped between them and took Skip by the arm. "Let's go down the road to the hamburger joint and bring back the lunch. By that time the genius will have solved everything." This brought Malloy's angry stare, but he said nothing and Sanderson and Skip Hudson walked over to where the Lotus coupe was parked.

As they drove away, Skip said, "I can't understand what made him so sore."

"Les likes to do everything himself. Haven't you ever noticed that? You watch him when we load the cars. He'll have to back the truck just so and lower the ramp just so and he'll even help push the cars in and check every detail." He shook his head. "A man gets that way when he begins to think that he can do everything better than someone else. But the day will come when he won't be able to do things like that, when he'll get into a situation where it'll be up to the peasants to do for him and then he's liable to crack up."

Skip looked at Sandy Sanderson. "You don't like Mr. Malloy, do you?"

Sanderson laughed. "Skip, after you've worked at Jim Vale's for awhile you're going to find that no one really likes anyone else." He reached the highway and accelerated the car, quickly pulling into traffic. "I understand you worked awhile for Volkswagen. Well, you don't have anything like that in their shops. The reason is simple: everything is on a fixed scale. It costs a poor man the same for a valve job as it does a rich one, and any mechanic can work on the car as well as the next one. But not at Vale's. He wants car owners to single out mechanics and it makes primadonnas of them. Pretty soon they just can't get along with each other." He glanced at Skip. "It's the same with drivers. You haven't met Phil Osgood, have you?" Skip shook his head. "Phil's around twenty-one. Real wild. The yellow car is his. Five engines blown in five races. It's a miracle he hasn't killed himself; he goes like a nut. But it's all a part of the Vale team strategy, Skip. Phil's sent out to break up the opposition by going like Jack-the-Bear. He usually lasts twenty laps while Malloy and I hang back in fifth or sixth, saving the cars. Then when Phil blows up, he's usually suckered someone else into the mess, and we move up into the money."

"You don't like Mr. Vale either," Skip said, coming into this new knowledge.

"Mr. Vale? Why, he's a sweetheart," Sanderson said. He pulled into a Giant Orange place and got out to order.

Chapter 3

A SPEEDSTER'S TRAGEDY

ANNE BECHEL was one of three girls employed by Vale Automotive; the other two were mature, married, and worked in the bookkeeper's office. From this Skip Hudson surmised that Jim Vale did not like to hire women, young or otherwise.

He ate lunch four times with Anne; they went out front, sat down on the curbing around the garden, and talked. Skip liked it.

Les Malloy didn't. When Skip came in, he said, "Hereafter eat your lunch in your own department."

Skip stopped and turned around and looked at Malloy; it was in his mind to tell him where to go because he hadn't been making an every day thing of having lunch with Anne Bechel.

It wasn't as though he had a romance going and he felt like telling Malloy so, but the Englishman had that go-ahead-and-you're-fired look in his eye, so Skip said nothing and went back to work.

He cashed his fourth pay check and put the money in his wallet; the other three he banked because his mother and Otto wanted it that way and because he secretly agreed that thrift was a good thing. He agreed with a lot of the things they told him to do, but often as not he'd keep this from them and argue and balk because he wanted to show his independence.

It was the same when they gave him a lecture; he could seem to let it go in one ear and out the other, as though it were somehow shameful to admit they were right, but secretly he weighed the advice and generally followed it.

Jim Vale's rules were the same; there were a lot of them, like coming to work and leaving work with clean hands, face, and clothes. Vale felt it was a poor advertisement to have his mechanics looking like grease monkeys. There was dirt all right, but the customer never saw it.

Jim Vale didn't like to have his employees picking up traffic tickets; you pick up two and he let you go. It was his opinion that people trusted his men with their cars, expensive cars, and he didn't want them to even think that irresponsible people were handling them.

One evening, when Skip and his family were having dinner and they were about through, Otto Hansen said, "How goes the job now, Skip?"

"Well, the pay is good." Then he felt a burst of honesty. "But I'd as soon take a cut and come back to Volkswagen." He looked at Otto quickly. "I'm not going to, though. As long as I do my work, Malloy and Jim Vale have no complaints."

"A man should be happy enough to whistle while he works," Otto said.

"Les Malloy says that Jim Vale is going to let me drive. Just to run-in some of the cars, that's all."

Skip's mother looked up. "I don't think you should do that." And before he could ask why not, she said, "I can't give you a reason, but it sounds like the start of something. And I'm not going to claw your shirt and cry and discuss the danger with you. Otto has long ago convinced me that it's more dangerous to drive in traffic." She reached out and touched his arm. "Skip, I want you to think about it."

"She means carefully," Otto said. "You know what she means."

Skip nodded and pushed his plate back; he recognized Otto's tone, which he used when he meant business. "It takes awhile for things to soak into my thick skull," Skip said, "but everybody at Vale's works for just the money. Sure, they do a good job because he demands it and no one wants to lose their job. His labor rate is higher than any independent in town, but he never lacks for customers. Some of the men in the shop say that Jim Vale has always gypped the customer of ten cents out of every dollar he charged, but I haven't seen any of it. But I can understand why you didn't want to work for him, Otto; you just wouldn't have got along at all."

"There isn't anything in the world exactly as a man wants it to be," Otto said, "but he tries to make the best of what he has." He got up. "Want to work on the boat for an hour or so?"

"Sure," Skip said and kissed his mother quickly as he passed her chair.

Malloy brought one of the older cars along on Skip's fourth overtime weekend in a row at Fawndale, and just from the way he acted, Skip knew that he was going to get his chance to drive. The car was a Cooper with a two liter Climax engine, a good car two years ago, but outclassed by newer, lighter, and more powerful machines.

Sanderson drove with Skip as a passenger, showing him how the shift worked, and demonstrating good driving technique. Then there was that heart-pounding ten minutes while Skip suited up in coveralls, got in the car and had the straps adjusted. Sanderson, with patience, again went through the matters of engine revolutions and shift pattern. Then he got into his own car, waved, revved up and left the pits with smoking tires.

Skip was driving a work-horse, a car used by many drivers to practice in before the races, and although no one had ever competed in the car, it was as fast as the one Sanderson was driving.

Hitting the starter button, Skip heard the overhead cam Ford engine sputter to life; it ran raggedly on three cylinders until he boosted the revs up to four thousand; then it ran smoothly on all four. He eased the shift lever into the starting gear, dropped the clutch and was immediately pushed back into his seat. His driving position was nearly supine; he was incredibly close to the road and he had never driven a car that accelerated so rapidly. Yet somehow it was not too different from his Austin Healey, only smaller and much quicker. Skip made his shift to second and kept on building speed, listening to the rising, smooth rip of the exhaust. A glance at the rev counter showed the needle straight up, seventy-five hundred revs; he made his shift to third and followed Sanderson into the first turn, a sweeping, banked turn that could be safely taken by an expert at 110 miles an hour.

They were not going that fast, Skip knew; probably eighty-five or so; he had no way of knowing because the only instruments he had were the rev counter, oil pressure, temperature gauge, and water temperature.

The Cooper, unlike his Healey, showed no tendency to slide; it followed the line Skip steered like a strip of paint and he was amazed at how smoothly the car rode, much better than his Healey. It seemed that he floated along, propelled by the small, but fantastically strong engine.

Sanderson had warned him not to down-shift for the corners; drivers rarely did this to kill their speed because the disc brakes were strong enough and would never fade. He watched Sanderson's brake lights go on at the last moment, crushed the pedal, and would have been thrown forward had not it been for the shoulder harness. The Cooper slowed as though it had hit some flexible barrier, and at the apex of the corner, Skip slipped the shift lever into second, banged on the throttle and shot out into a brief straight leading to the S-curves.

Skip knew that Sanderson was holding the speeds to safe limits, taking good lines through all the corners, and demonstrating good driving techniques, but it seemed to Skip that they were flying around the course. On the back straight, Sanderson turned on the tap and a glance at the rev counter showed seven thousand in fifth gear, which was in the neighborhood of 140 miles an hour. Yet the Cooper handled easily, with no vices, no tendency to wander; Skip had never driven so fine a car, so responsive, so delicate to handle.

They circulated twenty times; he had really lost count, and then Sanderson raised his hand to signal that they were going into the pits. Skip followed him in and shut off, then sat in the car gently patting the cowling and grinning like a fool.

Sanderson came over and said, "You like it?"

"Like WOW! Daddy, buy it for me." Skip laughed, unsnapped his harness and got out. Les Malloy was standing there with a clipboard; he had a page filled with his precise writing.

"Now we tell you what you did wrong," he said.

"Just about everything, I suppose," Skip said.

"Actually no," Malloy admitted. "You see, anyone who can handle a sports car quite well can soon learn to drive machinery like this. Of course everything is more sudden. The brakes are five times as effective, and you'll have to learn to use your acceleration better coming out of the corners." He checked his sheet. "I noticed that you did all your braking in a straight line before you entered the turn. Now with the newest suspension systems you can break right up to the center of the turn and still maintain control, providing you don't lock your wheels." He glanced at Sanderson. "I don't think it's too wise to teach him wrong, old boy."

"I was trying to give him a nice, safe ride!" Sandy snapped, then blew out a long breath and lit a cigarette.

Skip looked from one to the other then said, "I wish you guys wouldn't bicker. Remember, I'm in my formative years."

They both stared, then broke out laughing and the tension between them eased off. They talked about driving, about technique, and finally it was nearly time to load the cars. Skip handled the Cooper very gently, feeling almost as though he'd just bought it for himself.

He rode back to town with Sanderson and they talked about cars and drivers. At Vale's place they unloaded the cars, locked up, and then Skip got in his Healey and drove home.

Otto was watching television and when Skip came in the back way he turned it off and joined him in the kitchen, where the boy's mother was setting out the supper she had kept warm.

"Have a good day?" Otto asked.

"Sure did, Pop!"

"Aaahh," Otto said. "You got to drive, huh?"

"Just the 'work-horse.' A two year old Cooper." He tried to sound casual, but he couldn't hold it in and he bubbled over with it, spewing it all out, the thrill, the new excitement of driving the car.

Otto Hansen nodded and now and then made a comment, for he as a young man had watched the great, prewar might of the Mercedes-Benz and Auto-Union spread their aura of invincibility across Europe.

And it was Otto who kept reminding Skip to interrupt his enthusiasm long enough to eat his supper; he had a way of gently pushing that did not arouse resentment. "Since you've been gone all day, I don't suppose you've had a chance to look at the sports pages," Otto said. He got up, went into the living room, and came back with the paper, opening it to the page he wanted. There, wedged in between some football photos, was a picture of a badly mangled Lotus 23 with three course marshals trying to pry the driver out of the wreckage.

"That's Phil Osgood," Otto said. "He tried to get through turn nine at Riverside a little faster than everyone else. Right now he's in the Los Angeles hospital with a tube up his nose, a broken leg and collar bone, and some pretty serious internal injuries." He put his hand over the paper and made Skip look at him. "This happened yesterday morning. Now I want you to do something for me. I want you to ask Jim Vale if his giving permission for you to drive had anything to do with Osgood's accident."

"Gosh, how could it, Otto?"

"Ask him. Osgood will be out of racing for the rest of this season. Someone would have to take his place, some wild young man like Phil Osgood who'd drive too fast and take chances because he'd been convinced he was a hero."

"Aw, Pop, you don't think—?"

"Will you ask him?"

"Yes," Skip said seriously, "I'll ask him."

Otto Hansen seemed relieved; he sagged back in his chair and smiled. "Now, a young lady has been on the phone three times."

"Ohmygosh!" Skip said and bolted for the foyer.

"Thank God he's young," Otto said.

His wife looked questioningly at him. "I don't see an advantage."

"Girls still have the power to take his mind off cars."

Anne Bechel lived on a quiet side street near the Methodist Church. After showering and running a razor over his face, Skip picked her up and they went downtown to a movie. Afterwards he drove to a drive-in near the center of town and parked, blinking his lights to attract a carhop.

She took their order and they sat there, talking and not paying any attention to anyone else. Then someone rocked the back of Skip's car and he looked around. Larry Wise and two friends stood there and Skip said, "Aw, come on, Larry, knock it off."

Larry came to the door and leaned. "How's the big man with the job?" The other two went around to the other side and waited, smiling foolishly.

"What's eating you?" Skip asked.

"I got aced out at Vale's and I wonder if you did it?"

"How could I do it, Larry? Until I saw you at Vale's a month or so ago I hadn't said 'Boo' to you since school."

"We were never chums," Larry said and bumped the car door with his knee.

"So what? Two hundred in the class and I've got to be a pal to everybody?"

"Don't give me mathematics," Larry said. He was lanky and dark and he seemed to be eternally brooding, constantly displeased; it was in his eyes and the quick, darting motions of his hands when he talked.

"I'm not giving you anything," Skip said flatly. "You came up to me so why don't you just bug out and find someone else to bother."

Larry reared back in mock surprise and hurt. "Every hand raised against me. Now is that right, Skip? Suppose a thing like that got into the Russians' hands? Wouldn't that sound keen on Radio Free Europe? The caste system in America."

"Oh, come off it," Skip said. "You want a burger or somethin'?"

"Bribery?" Larry asked, smiling. He looked at his friends. "How about that?"

Skip sighed. "Do you always take what people say and twist it around to suit you?" He started to climb out of the car but Larry pushed him back.

"Don't get horsy now."

"Horsy?" Skip's temper put an edge to his voice. "Get out and leave us alone."

Larry spoke to his friends. "He's gettin' hot, isn't he? How'd you like to drag for pink slips?"

"Drop—"

"Ah, ah!" Larry said, holding up his hand. "Unkind thoughts there. I'm just looking for a little diversion on a dull evening and you've got to spoil it by talking hard."

"Don't kid me. You're hunting trouble."

"Didn't I tell you to watch where you parked this thing? But would you listen to old Larry? No, you've got to play it big."

He reached inside, trying to find the door handle, then stopped when one of the other boys on the other side of the car said, "Hey, Larry!" He pointed toward the drive-in; a woman inside was talking on the telephone and watching them all the time. "She's sending up a flare for the cops!"

"Yeah, let's bug out," Larry said. He slapped Skip on the head. "See you, kid." Then they dashed for the pickup and howled out, rear tires protesting.

The waitress came out with their shakes and burgers;

she hooked the tray onto the door and said, "That Larry, he's going to get it some day. But good!"

Then she went to tend another car and Skip handed Anne her food. "Don't look so worried," he said.

A police car drove in and two officers went inside, spoke to the woman, then came over to Skip Hudson's car. "We don't want a rumble tonight," the officer said. "If I were you I'd eat and go home." He looked them over carefully and made his judgments. "We know Larry. One of these days he'll turn twenty-one and he'll end up in jail."

Then they got back into their car and drove across the street, parking in the dark shadows alongside a farm implement company.

"I wouldn't want their job," Anne said. "Nothing but trouble!" She sipped her shake. "Skip, are you going to stay on at Vale's?"

He looked at her curiously. "Well, what's wrong with Vale's? I mean, it's a good job. I don't think anyone there has a right to kick about their wages. I started at two and a quarter an hour. If I pan out, I can make three and a half or four. You know, that's good money."

"But is it what you want to do, Skip?"

He shrugged. "I really don't know what I want to do. Sometimes I think that Otto is right, that I should go to college, but I don't know what to major in. And I like working, earning my own money. Since my dad died years ago we've always had to be careful with money. Not that we were poor, but we just couldn't rush right out and buy the first thing we saw." He smiled. "And it's good for a guy's pride to be earning his own bread."

"Larry doesn't work, does he?"

He looked at her, surprised that she'd mention him. "No, he's not working. It's his own fault because he's always got a chip on his shoulder."

"I wonder why?"

Skip shrugged. "His father, I guess." He fell into a thoughtful silence. "It's too bad Vale didn't hire him because Larry needs a job. A guy like Larry can have too much free time on his hands. He ought to go into the army or something."

He finished his shake and burger and waited for her. Then the waitress came out for the tray; she took his money and brought his change, nodding to indicate the darker spot in the parking lot.

"Your buddy's back," she said and Skip looked and saw that Larry had brought his pickup in through the alley and was parked there, waiting.

"He must be out of his mind," Anne said, and waited for Skip to make the decision.

"Why don't I put you in a cab? There's no sense in you getting mixed up in this."

She shook her head. "I don't want to see you get involved with him, Skip."

He laughed without humor. "Neither do I."

The carhop was still standing there. "Look, why don't I phone the police and have them radio the car and—"

"You can't arrest him for parking in the parking lot," Skip said, drumming his fingers gently on the steering wheel.

"And we can't sit here all night either," Anne said. "Skip, why don't we leave? Just pull out and leave. He'll have to make the first move, won't he?"

"Yep, that makes sense," Skip said and started the car. He checked to see if her seat belt was fastened, and backed out.

Anne said, "Skip, we're not going to race, are we?"

"Not a chance," he assured her. "I'm not going to be hauled into traffic court for anybody." He stopped at the street edge to let some traffic pass. Then he eased out and had hardly pulled into the proper lane when Larry shot out, tires smoking. He had given no regard to traffic and some people in a Chevrolet had to lock their wheels to keep from hitting him broadside.

Larry roared after the Healey, exhausts blasting, and the police car pulled out, red light and siren on.

"Now he's done it," Skip said and slowed his car, pulling over to the side of the road. He watched Larry and the police car in his rear-view mirror, expecting Larry to kill his speed and pull over.

But he shot by, speeding up, making a race of it.

"The darned fool!" Skip said and stopped the car completely. He opened the door on her side. "Bail out! I want to find out what's going to happen."

"Not without me."

"Don't be a fool! I don't want to take a chance on your getting hurt."

"You're wasting time, I refuse to bail out," she said and closed the door.

Larry and the police car were far down Willow Pass now and Skip made his decision; he snapped the Healey into first gear and shot away, tires chirping each time he made a shift. In his mind he was calling Larry some names he never said aloud; the fool was going to land in jail this time for sure, and people would say that was where he'd been heading all the time because he was full of resentment and mischief and some of the things he'd done weren't pranks.

A glance at the speedometer showed Skip that they were doing seventy and still the police car and Larry stayed in the distance; he was barely holding his own with them.

Oh, what a fool, Skip thought, and wondered what it was in young people that kept them from ever admitting they could be wrong. He knew what it was like because he'd felt that way, and there had been times in his life when he'd rather have taken a beating than admit to his mother and Otto that he'd been wrong.

But it was something a boy had to outgrow if he was ever going to be a man at all. Skip supposed Larry was sore because the police had arrived and spoiled his fun; it would be something like that, some frustration that would set him off.

Ahead, Larry braked heavily, tires squealing, and slid the pickup around a corner, almost losing it. The police followed, siren wailing, red bulb on the roof rotating fingers of light.

Skip had to brake heavily and the Austin Healey took the corner with a slight sliding motion. Skip found that he had gained on Larry and the police, but Larry was letting out the power of the hopped-up engine and pulling away from the patrol car.

Skip could guess where Larry was heading, up Laurel canyon where the road was a series of sharp switchbacks and the power of his pickup would soon outrun the police car.

The road started to climb, a series of gentle S's, and they were going ninety miles an hour now, with Larry taking all the road, sliding the pickup clear across at each bend. The patrol car had to slow down, which let him pull farther away.

Skip would have had no difficulty passing the police and staying with Larry because the Healey, designed for sports car racing, had the acceleration and the handling to catch him, but Skip wouldn't pull in front of the patrol car.

So they wound up the mountain as fast as the police dared to go; their car still had the siren and red light flashing and Skip stayed behind them.

Then suddenly the police car was braking heavily, skidding sideways in the road. Skip managed to stop in time and not hit them. He saw, in the headlight's glare, and in the spotlight the police flashed about, the gash in the wooden guardrail alongside the road. Quickly he backed out of the way, parked, and got out his flashlight and fire extinguisher; the police were shining lights down into the ravine and Larry's pickup was there, upside down, the front wheels still turning.

"Stay in the car," Skip said to Anne and slid down the steep, brush-choked slope with one patrolman; the other was in the car, calling a wrecker and an ambulance over the radio.

Skip reached the pickup first and tried to wrench open the door, but it was damaged and he could not budge it. The side window was broken on the other side so he went around, put his arm in, and rolled it down. Larry was unconscious and had a cut on his head; his two friends were dazed and hanging upside down by their seatbelts.

Swinging his feet and hips inside, Skip managed to kick while the officer pulled and together they got the door open. The other policeman came down and they got the three boys out of the damaged truck.

Larry regained consciousness as he was pulled out. Somehow the balance of the wrecked pickup was disturbed and it rolled farther down the ravine, coming to rest on its side.

The three young men were dazed and bruised and all cut a little by the glass from the broken side window; the police made them sit quietly until the ambulance got there and one of the officers went down and shut off the lights, which were still burning on the pickup.

Larry rubbed his head and stared at a spot between his shoes. A policeman stood nearby, watching all of them. He said, "Don't you guys ever learn?" Then he looked at Skip Hudson. "What's your part in this?"

Now that he'd been asked, Skip found that he really didn't know. He supposed, because Larry had been after him in the first place, that this was somehow partly his fault, but he couldn't bring himself to take any of the blame for it.

"I guess I don't have any," he said, then cocked his head and listened to the ambulance come up the hill. Larry and his friends were taken up and put inside and the ambulance turned around and started down, siren growling in its throat.

Skip went to his car, started it, turned around, and followed the ambulance down. Toward town he saw a lighted phone booth, stopped and called home to tell his mother what had happened and that he was going on to the hospital. Before he hung up, Anne said, "I'll go with you."

He nodded and told his mother to phone her house, then hung up and got back in his car.

Parkside Hospital was across town and he swung north on Willow Pass, caught the freeway and went down to the main boulevard overpass. When they got to the hospital, they parked and went in to the main desk. The nurse on duty told them to go to central receiving, as the accident cases went there first.

Ten minutes later they found it and asked about Larry.

The nurse there checked her cards. Yes, he had been detained; she'd check with the doctor on duty. Fifteen minutes later she came back and told them to go to the main desk again.

As they walked down the corridor, Skip said, "I'm glad I'm not an accident case!"

The desk nurse gave them Larry's room number and they went into one of the wings, walking along, looking at door numbers. They finally found the right one and a doctor stepped out, looking surprised to find them there.

"Are you relatives?" he asked.

"No," Skip said. "Can we see him?"

"Sure, he's just bruised and sprained a little. Go on in, but don't stay long." He smiled and walked on down the hall; he seemed to be a man on urgent business.

Larry was in bed, a bandage wound around his head, and the cuts on his arms painted a bright red. He looked at Skip and said, "Everything I had was in that car." He made an idle, futile motion with his hand. "Did you come here to laugh or something?"

"I don't think there's anything to laugh about," Skip said. "I'm glad you're not seriously hurt. Your car rolled on down aways after you got out."

"I know," Larry said dully. "I came to just after you climbed in and kicked the door open." He looked at Skip for a moment. "I don't know whether or not I'd have done that for you. I just thought I'd tell you that to keep the record straight."

"What do you do, keep score or something?" Skip asked.

The door opened and the two policemen came in. One looked at Larry and grinned. "Well, Stirling Moss, you look all right. One of these days we'll be sliding you into one of the reefer cribs at the morgue and calling your folks to come and identify you." Then he looked at Skip and Anne. "Are you following us or are we following you?" He took out a pencil and a notebook. "Let me have your names and addresses." He wrote them down and turned his attention to Larry.

"Wise, you're in trouble this time. Failure to make a proper stop, failure to yield right of way, failure to heed red light and siren, speeding, driving with undue caution. You're going to have a big lump on your head when the judge hits you with the book."

Larry sneered. "Man, we're really stamping out crime tonight, aren't we?"

The policemen didn't think it was funny, because the quiet one said, "Sonny, isn't there anything you take seriously?"

"He doesn't mean to be a wise guy," Skip said, and

then wondered what had made him say that. Thinking about it, he realized he understood how it was with Larry, wanting to do what was right and generally doing what was wrong.

"He knows he's goofed," Skip said. "You don't have to remind him of it."

The talkative policeman said, "What are you, a psychiatrist or something? I have to deal with these punks every day."

The other policeman said, "Let it go, Ralph. You've made your point." He turned to the door and held it open, and Ralph turned and went out. Then the policeman winked and said, "Tomorrow morning the sun's liable to shine. Take it easy."

After he closed the door, Larry said, "What did he mean by that?" Then he looked at Skip. "And I'll do my own explaining when I feel like it. Understand?"

"I understood all right, Larry. You want me to call your folks and tell them what happened?"

"Let them read it in the papers."

Skip Hudson's face grew dark with anger. He went to the bed and put his hand on Larry's chest and his fingers trembled. "Listen, Muscle-Head, I've felt like telling my mother to go jump a lot of times, but I never said it. We all get like this, but you'd better get something straight right now. The thing to do, the right thing, is to tell your folks what happened. All night long you've been piling one mistake on another, and it won't improve anything to make another. You didn't need to pick a beef with me. Or to come back, or to take out after me. You could have stopped when the cops buzzed you and taken a chewing and had it over with. But you had to go the whole way. OK, so you've gone. Now be smart. I'll call your folks and I won't sugar coat anything. What's your phone number?"

Larry thought about it, then said, "Highgate 4-8964."

Skip gave Anne a dime. "There's a phone booth at the end of the hall." She went out and Skip stepped back away from Larry's bed, still angry.

"What happened to Skinny and Hooker?" Larry asked.

"The two that were with you? They cut out. What did you expect them to do? You could have killed them. They're probably home, glad to be away from you."

"They could have come in to see how I was," Larry said.

"You figure they owed you that?" Skip shook his head. "No one owes you anything, Larry. Because you don't do anything, that's why."

"What's there to do?" Larry asked, his voice rising.

Anne came back in and smiled. "Your dad wasn't home but he'll be right over."

"You're kidding," Larry said. "This is his bowling night. Tomorrow night it's lodge and the next night it's billiards. Wednesdays night he stays home and Thursday he plays poker. Big man." He looked at Anne. "What do you lie for anyway? I know this is his bowling night."

"I know," Anne said. "When I couldn't get an answer, I called a friend of mine who lives on your street. She told me the name of the bowling alley and I called him there. He's coming over."

"You went to a lot of trouble for me," Larry said quietly.

"It wasn't any trouble," Anne told him. "Skip, we should go."

"OK." They turned to the door as the doctor poked his head in.

"I thought I told you not to build a nest in here. Leaving? OK." He smiled and went on down the hall, and Anne and Skip went out to the car.

As they got in, she said, "I'm glad we stopped in to see him, Skip. I don't think he has anybody, really. You know?"

"Yeah," Skip said and started the car.

Chapter 4

WEEKEND RACING AT FAWNDALE

It was after midnight when Skip pulled his car into the garage and went into the house; his mother and Otto Hansen were waiting for him. Otto got up and turned off the television set while Skip hung his coat in the closet.

His mother was the first to speak. "Skip, is this Larry a friend of yours?"

"No, I don't really even know him," Skip said, sprawling in an easy chair.

Otto took off his glasses and laid them aside. "Then I don't think we really understand your concern, Skip."

"Well, I don't either, Otto. I wish I did. And it just isn't young people sticking together or anything like that." He was silent and rubbed his hands together a moment before going on. "I guess it's just that he's in trouble and didn't have anyone to turn to, anyone who'd understand without asking a lot of questions. You know, I've had my own troubles and never said anything about them. It wasn't that I wanted to keep them to myself, but somehow you just never do a very good job of explaining to older people. Your reasons never sound very good to them and then you have one mistake piled on another." He looked from one to the other. "Does this make any sense to you?"

"Yes it does," his mother said. "What do you want to do, Skip?"

He shrugged and kicked off his shoes. "I guess I want to try and help him. I don't think his old man will. He'll ask a lot of questions that can't be answered and Larry'll feel just as much out on a limb as he does now. He flung his arms out. "Heck, we don't even understand the problem most of the time. That's Larry's trouble. He didn't have to tell me. I just knew it. Anne did too."

"How much trouble is he in?" Otto asked.

Skip rolled his eyes dramatically. "The judge is liable to brain him with the book, according to the police."

"Does he have a job?" Otto asked.

Skip shrugged. "I'd say no, but that's just a guess. He doesn't act like a kid with a job." He pried himself out of the chair and remembered to pick up his shoes. "But I guess I'll try to help him. It just seems like the right thing to do."

"If you start to get in over your head," Otto said, "be sure to ask me for a hand. All right?"

"Sure, Otto. Good night."

The next day, Skip asked Les Malloy for two hours off and went into town to the county building to talk to the probation officer, who made it plain that Larry Wise was in trouble. The judge was not liable to show consideration unless Larry had some guarantee of employment, and even then he'd have to report regularly to the probation officer until he'd proven to the court's satisfaction that he had changed his ways.

The job, Skip was assured, was most important, and he left, mulling that over in his mind.

He thought about it for two days, then asked Les Malloy for permission to see Jim Vale. Vale was on a long-distance call when Malloy came in; he waited until Vale was through, then told him that young Hudson wanted to see him.

Vale frowned and said, "What about? You know I don't like to be bothered, Les." He waved his hand impatiently. "All right, bring him in. But you stick around. I want this short and sweet."

Then he leaned back in his chair while Malloy went to the shop to get Skip. As soon as they came back in, Vale motioned for Skip to close the door, then said, "All right, what's on your mind today?"

"I have something I want to talk over with you, Mr. Vale." He quickly related the events leading up to Larry Wise's accident and arrest.

Vale listened carefully, then said, "Sure, I remember him. The boy in the pickup. I remember now reading about his accident in the papers. They ought to publish names. These kids are shown too much consideration." He looked steadily at Skip. "So why is it skin off your nose?"

"I want to help him."

Vale looked at Malloy, then back to Skip. "What for?"

"Because he needs it."

"He doesn't deserve it," Vale snapped.

Skip shook his head. "Mr. Vale, I just can't decide a thing like that."

"You've decided that he needs help. Why can't you decide that he doesn't?" He looked at Malloy and laughed, proud of the logic he had displayed. "Look, you've a nice kid, Skip. Got a lot on the ball. This Larry is a punk. He's headed for jail and the sooner he gets there, the better off the town will be. So just forget it, huh?"

Malloy said, "Mr. Vale, can't you see that he can't do that?"

Vale had turned to some paper work, certain that he had settled the matter and when Malloy spoke, he looked up, annoyance on his face.

"All right, kid, I'll give it to you straight. You work for me and I like your work. But when a man works for me, he takes my orders and I'm telling you to forget this Larry Whatshisname."

He picked up his pen to write, but stopped when Malloy said, "Jim, you're daring him to defy you and yet making it clear to him that if he does you'll sack him. I think he's right."

"Oh, you do, do you?" Vale's eyes were like polished marbles, expressionless. "You're on his side, huh?"

"Because he's right," Les Malloy said. "Jim, on the job you can make him jump your way, but off duty his business is his own." He smiled to soften Vale's temper. "Think about it a minute, Jim. We're talking about this young man's self-respect. You don't want bums working for you and here you have a chap batting for what's right and you're blaming him for it. It doesn't make sense, Jim, and that surprises me because you're one of the most sensible men I know."

"Are you buttering me up?" Vale asked.

"I've got better sense than that," Malloy said. "But I'm asking you to consider both sides of this, Jim. The boy's right and you ought to be thankful he cares enough to be in here right now. He doesn't want to make you sore and neither do I, but—"

Vale turned his anger on Les Malloy. "All right, knock it off!" He pointed his pen at Skip Hudson. "I'm going to spell this out for you: Larry is a punk. He's got a rap coming. Is that plain enough for you?"

"Yes, sir, but you're insisting that you do what *you* think is right. Now I have to do the same thing, Mr. Vale."

"All right, one more word and you're through!" Vale said. "I say that boy gets what's coming to him and that's that!"

"No, sir, it's not," Skip said. "I've said my word, and I'm fired, so I'll finish it before I leave. Larry Wise may deserve punishment, Mr. Vale, but only at the hands of the people he's offended. He doesn't deserve punishment from others."

"By jove!" Malloy said and applauded softly and drew Vale's brief stare.

Vale spent a full minute looking at Skip Hudson, then a laugh burst from him and he threw his pen aside and tipped his chair back. "Skip, you've got nerve all right. I can't help but admire anyone who sticks with what he believes."

"I didn't come in to get in an argument or to butt heads," Skip told him. "But after talking to the probation officer, there isn't much that can be done for Larry until he has a job."

Vale's eyebrows shot up. "You want *me* to give him a job? You're out of your head."

"Don't you think you can handle him?" Malloy asked.

"Whose side are you on? And keep out of this."

"You asked me to stay," Malloy said. "Skip's got a point. You could find something for Larry. If Skip could come in here and go out on a limb for him, it won't hurt you to climb the tree."

"I don't need advice," Vale said, but he made a wry face and pulled at his ear. "All right, Skip, if a man's as determined as you are, I'll go along with him for awhile. We'll find something here for this—this kid."

"Thanks, Mr. Vale," Skip said.

"Thanks? You've ruined my day. Now beat it and get to work."

Malloy walked back with him and as they neared Malloy's office, he said, "I didn't think the old boy would back down. Fact is, you struck his funny bone or else you'd be sacked by now. Even though I think you were right, I wouldn't advise you doing it again."

Skip shook his head. "Well, Mr. Malloy, I don't think the judge would take my word that Larry's been promised a job. Mr. Vale will have to appear or sign a—"

"Oh, I say, that'll be jolly," Malloy said, and stepped into his office.

That evening Skip called Al Cady, the probation officer, and told him about the arrangement he had made for Larry with Jim Vale, and Cady said he'd take the matter up with Judge Scanlon.

Skip put the matter out of mind because he was busy at the shop. That weekend he went to Monterey and the Laguna Seca sports car races as part of Vale's pit crew.

It was the first event Skip had attended as part of the team; Vale had three Lotus 23s there, and a work-horse car which Sanderson inconveniently slid into the hay bales, damaging it so badly that Skip and two other mechanics worked half the night to get it running again.

The body was badly bent, some of the frame tubes had to be replaced, and the right front end had to be rebuilt from spares in the parts truck.

There was an excitement to a race weekend, even before the paying spectators arrived. Concession people moved in, spotting soft drink and hot dog stands around the hilly course. In the pit area, banners and flags were strung on high wires and the cars, drivers, and crews with their repair vans arrived early Friday. By afternoon it was all noise, engines being tuned in and drivers out on the course, tearing around, trying to master the tricky corners.

Sandy Sanderson and Les Malloy were scheduled to drive two of the cars but neither man knew who was going to drive the third, and Jim Vale wasn't saying. There was a platform built on top of the car van and a beach umbrella kept off the sun; Vale perched up there with his bathing trunks and field glasses, like a general surveying everything before the eve of battle.

Late Friday afternoon Vale called on the megaphone for Skip, who climbed the ladder to his boss' "quarterdeck." Vale handed Skip the keys to his Jaguar sedan. "Clean up, change your clothes, and drive in to San Francisco airport. Meet the TWA flight from London. Pick up three passengers."

Skip pushed back his surprise. "Yes, sir. Who'll I be—"

"Just go to the reservation desk, identify yourself and tell them I sent you. They have instructions." He reached out and gave Skip a slap on the shoulder. "Now get going. And don't pick up any tickets."

"Yes, sir!" He turned to go down the ladder but stopped when Vale spoke.

"And if anyone asks you where you're going, tell them you're running an errand for me. OK?"

"OK," Skip said.

Since the racecourse was on a military reservation, no one was permitted to camp overnight; everyone stayed in town at motels and the MP's guarded the cars and equipment. Skip unlocked Vale's car, started it and drove the seven miles into town. When he pulled into the motel and parked, Sanderson and Malloy came up, both in swim trunks.

Malloy said, "I saw the car and thought the old man was coming in. What's up? Did he say when we were going to practice?"

"Nope. I didn't hear anything."

Sandy said, "He's not sore because I bent the—"

Skip shook his head. "He didn't act sore. Besides, the car's all fixed."

"Where you going?" Malloy asked.

Skip opened his mouth to tell him, then remembered Vale's remark. "A flunky job," he said and went into the unit to bathe and change clothes. Then he drove away in the Jaguar, stopping down the road to fill the gas tank, and went on to San Francisco.

The trip took him a little more than an hour and a half, driving as steadily as the traffic would permit. He pulled into the limousine parking area, paid the attendant and went inside to check on the plane's arrival.

Jim Vale came in early, invited Sandy Sanderson and Les Malloy to dinner, and then worried them because he was so jolly. He ordered personally from the chef and examined the wine with care before selecting a 1948 vintage. Sandy and Malloy kept looking at each other, wondering what it was all about.

Finally Vale said, "It's too bad about Phil Osgood. I needed him this weekend to tiger around and burn up the opposition." He lit a cigarette and looked from one to the other. "If you two were fast enough I wouldn't need Osgood, would I?"

"You've got no complaints," Sanderson said bluntly. "What's all this about, Jim?"

"You want to know? I'm putting you both on the fence for the Sunday event." He checked his wristwatch. "Skip's gone into San Francisco to pick up the drivers who will take your places." He paused to let it sink in. "I've got Phil Hill, Richie Ginther, and Dan Gurney. They're flying in from Europe. They're going to sit in the front row and when that flag drops they're going to charge off that grid, run off, and hide from everybody. And you two are going to see that they do it. Those cars will be checked and rechecked. There won't be any mechanical trouble, understand. If there is, you're hunting jobs. OK?"

Sanderson said nothing, but Les Malloy had something

on his mind. "No, it's not OK, Jim. You've always been a chap with a lot of cheek and I've admired that at times. But we're people, Jim, not something you can use and throw away." He pushed back his chair and stood up. "I'll stop around Monday morning for my check." He looked at Sandy Sanderson. "How about you, Sandy? Are you going to let him buy you or is there still something of yourself that you call your own?"

"By golly there is," Sanderson said and got up. "Have a nice weekend, Jim. I'll go with Les."

Vale showed his surprise. "You'd quit now? Look, I've got a race to win. At least you could supervise the pit crew. If you leave, who'll I get? I've got two mechanics who speak broken English and young Hudson. I thought you were reasonable men. It's only *this* race. You're still number one and two drivers. What the heck now."

"For how long?" Malloy asked, shaking his head. "No thanks, Jim. I've had it." He looked at Sanderson. "Coming, Sandy?"

"Sure, but where to?"

"Well," Malloy admitted, "I kind of thought I'd take the wife and kids to the beach, Sunday. Why don't you bring your wife and come along?"

"That's a good idea." Sandy reached into his pocket and tossed five dollars on the table. "Give that to the waitress, Jim; it'll make you feel like a big tipper."

Skip Hudson could never quite describe the drive back from the airport; the recollection of it was so heady that he had difficulty keeping it straight in his mind. They were in his car, three of the world's finest drivers, and he maintained a complete silence, content to listen to them talk about places, races, cars, and a lot of other things, most of which he didn't know much about.

When he arrived at the motel, he carried their luggage inside and saw that they were checked in. He left them after promising to let Jim Vale know they'd arrived. Just as he was getting in the car someone whistled and he looked around, right and left, to see who it was. Then he saw Jim Vale standing behind some large potted palms by the pool and he went over, wondering what Vale was doing acting like a detective.

Vale took Skip by the arm and hauled him out of sight. "Son, drive the car around by the end of the units and wait for me there. Go on now, and don't ask questions."

Skip went back to the car and did as he was told, parking alongside the last unit. A few minutes later Jim Vale opened the door and got in. "Drive someplace," he said and lit a cigarette as Skip pulled out into traffic. He went three blocks and then pulled into a drive-in.

"I haven't had any chow," he said by way of explanation.

"Sure, sure," Vale said. "Get what you want; it's on me." He said nothing more until the girl had taken Skip's order. "Boy, we're in a little bit of a fix here. Kind of unexpected, but that's the way these things are."

"I don't know what you're talking about, sir."

"I'm talking about Sandy and Les; they up and quit just because I hired three first-string drivers to race Sunday. Look, I counted on them to handle the pit work. That's why I brought Hermann and Luigi along; I figured Sandy and Les could handle anything." He wiped a hand across his mouth. "Boy, you just don't understand."

"No, I guess I don't. The cars are all right and Hermann and—"

"Sure, they're top men but you don't know these Grand Prix drivers, Skip. They've got to look good all the time. They've got their public to think of. And if they found out that my two best men had walked off they'd scratch their entry, get on a plane and go back to Europe. It cost me fifteen thousand to bring them here. I'm not going to lose that money."

"They'll find out, won't they?"

"Not if we play it smart," Vale said. "Skip, I'm putting you in charge of the cars and the pits. Cater to them. Hang on their every word. Listen to their complaints and comments. And keep your mouth shut because a man always seems to know more if he just nods and looks wise."

"That's not very honest, Mr. Vale. It would be better to level with them and hope—"

"I don't run a business on hope, boy. Now you do this my way. You've worked with Malloy and Sanderson nearly every weekend. You've driven enough to be able to test a car. You're a good mechanic with a nice pair of hands and good ears. So think out there and you'll come off like a rose." He reached out and gripped Skip's wrist. "Malloy's gone. I'll have to find a man or move one up. You can have Sanderson's place in the organization. A good salary and a car to drive. Heck, you've got talent for it. I'm offering you something most young men would jump at." He gave Skip's wrist a tug. "Now you fall out in the morning and take over, understand. I'll talk to Hermann and Luigi and they'll jump when you whistle.

A little extra in it for them, you know." He smiled and drew deeply on his cigarette. "You're going to be all right out there, kid. You can handle yourself. OK?"

"It's OK because there isn't any other choice," Skip said. "But I'd as soon not do it. Nothing's ever worked out for me when I pretend." The girl came with his cheeseburger and malted. He paid her and when she walked away, Skip said, "I'm beginning to understand your rules, Mr. Vale. You sort of make them up as you go along, huh?"

"Boy, I've had to. My father was a plumber's helper, and I never had a nickel of my own that I didn't work for. All my life it's been: 'Hey, kid, do this! Hey, kid, get the lead out! Hey, kid, be my flunky.' Well, I never liked it and I told myself that it wasn't going to be that way. I've learned to take care of myself and worry about the next guy if I have the time."

"About Larry Wise, Mr. Vale—I take it he starts to work Monday morning. Something like my old job. Not a flunky, as you put it."

Jim Vale laughed and slapped Skip on the shoulder. "Putting the squeeze on me, huh? All right, I don't mind. Sure, the punk's hired."

"His name is Larry Wise," Skip said evenly, trying to keep the resentment out of his voice.

"OK," Vale said, laughing. "Larry Wise. Now eat up and take me back. I've got continental racing drivers to squire around. You'll be on the course early?"

"By sun up," Skip said. "I'll slow time the cars around the course and have them warmed up for early practice."

"That's my boy," Vale said and leaned back in the seat, his mood expansive.

Hermann and Luigi had the company pickup, and a Honda 50 motorcycle, which was handy for dashing about the pits and racecourse. Skip took the motorcycle out when the sky was just turning pink. The air was very chilly and although he had on a warm coat, he was shivering by the time he reached the course and was admitted by the military police.

The van had a generator and lighting system, and he pulled the rope starter until it fired. Then he switched on some lights and took the canvas covers off the cars. Getting out the hydraulic jack, Skip raised the back of one car, plugged in the external power so as not to flatten the rather small battery, and started the car. He ran it, burbling and protesting, until the oil temperature started to rise, then let the rear end down, got in, strapped himself and eased onto the course, holding the car to five-thousand revolutions in gears as he climbed rapidly up past the start-finish line. He continued over a rise and down into a swale, the straightness of the road marred by a slight kink to the left. At the bottom there was a gentle left hand turn, then a long climbing sweep to the top of the hill; he used fourth gear, but still held the revs down. At the top he braked for another left hander; quickly the road dipped sharply into a series of left and right switchbacks. Then he was entering the downhill stretch, a long fast bend to the left, and at the bottom, another to the right. A short straight brought him to the hairpin turn and again to the straight leading past the start-finish.

Skip cracked on some more revolutions this time, for

the oil temperature was getting up to normal; he shifted at six thousand, listening to the tearing silk rip of the exhaust echo across the bowl of hills.

There was dew on the course and frost up on the hill where the sharp downhill S's were; the Lotus slid from side to side, but the tires bit in time and he rounded the left hander, going down in a long, gentle slide.

One more time around and then he saw headlights as cars and trucks entered the pit areas; other early ones coming out to get their expensive and delicate machinery ready.

He pulled into the pits, parked the Lotus, and warmed up what would have been Sanderson's car. The sun was an orange ball when he pulled onto the course. Soon steam rose from the blacktop and the frost under the trees on the hill started to melt.

After he had parked this car and started the other one, Vale's Jaguar pulled in, but Skip kept on working. He was letting the jack down and climbing in when Vale and Ginther came over and watched; he said nothing, just pulled onto the course, throttled up, shifted fast and went around and around, increasing his revs gradually until he was reading operating temperatures on all gauges. When he came around the hairpin for the last time, he pushed the revs on up to eight thousand on each shift, letting the acceleration slam him back, feeling the Lotus rocket up the hill like a dragster, the exhaust ripping. At the bottom of the hill he braked and slacked off, easing it around and then coming into the pits.

Vale was there; the others had taken the car and gone and Vale was smiling. "Very impressive," he said. "They took the car back in town to eat. Hermann and Luigi will be here soon. Everything all right?"

"Sure, until something breaks," Skip said. "When will they start practice?"

"Nine o'clock." Vale looked at his watch. "It's not quite seven thirty. These boys like to drive. So see that they use the work-horse until they're familiar with the course. When it comes to time trials, switch to the other cars and give them about a gallon and a half of gas. They don't want to pack any more weight around than they have to. If they get stuck out there on the course, send Hermann in the pickup." He puffed his cheeks and patted his stomach. "I'll be glad when today and tomorrow is over with."

Vale walked away; he saw someone he wanted to talk to, and Skip started the spare Lotus, warming it carefully on the jacks, but he didn't take it out on the course. Several other cars were circulating at high speed and since he had had no experience at all in traffic driving, he stayed in the pits, not wanting to risk bending the spare car.

Not after working so hard to fix it.

A few minutes before nine, Ginther and the others came back. Hermann and Luigi had already arrived and the drivers got into the cars to see how well they fit. Dan Gurney was very tall and the seat had to be changed to fit him, for a racing car was not like a sedan; a driver literally wore the car. Ginther, a small man in his early thirties with sun wrinkles around his eyes, needed some fitting, and when he was satisfied, he turned his head and looked at Hudson.

"Anything I ought to know?"

"Go," Skip said, making a pushing motion with his hands. Ginther grinned and put on his helmet, gave his shoulder harness a final tug and eased down the pit lane, blipping the throttle to keep the spark plugs from fouling up.

Then he roared out, leaving behind the aroma of castor oil and rubber. Hill left next and finally Gurney and Skip sat on the running board of the pickup truck and watched them circulate, increasing their speed until it seemed that they just couldn't go any faster.

But they would; they always seemed to hold something back. They were like that, in complete control all the time, always able to shave off another tenth of a second.

Practice ran until noon. Then the production car races began and the hillsides were crowded with spectators, their bright clothing like large flowers in the sun. When the cars were brought in, they were parked and covered; the pit crew would change tires and check them later.

Skip went over to one of the hot dog stands and bought his lunch. While he ate, he sat in the shade on a hillside and watched the MGs, the Porsches, and the Triumphs fight it out while a long Morgan Super-Sport led them all.

Racing was thunder noise and bright cars speeding past and the loud-speakers trying to drown them out as the announcers on each corner brought the distant action close. The excitement of it was everywhere, infecting everyone.

And Skip Hudson, sitting there in his white driving coveralls with VALE RACING TEAM on the back in bright letters, drew attention and comments. He liked it and chided himself for it because he wasn't a driver, yet he found it easy to pretend that he was, let them think that he was.

It wasn't a good thing to do and it bothered him because he just didn't get up and go back to the pits where he belonged. He finished his hot dogs and sipped his orange. A girl, passing behind him, said, "That must be Pedro Roderiguez; he's awfully young."

Skip knew who she meant; Roderiguez had been motorcycle champion of Mexico by the time he was fifteen, and was driving Grand Prix cars before he was old enough to get a state driver's license.

But that settled it; he took his orange and paper wrappers and went back to the pits, sitting on the pickup running board and watching the races from there. Hermann wanted to get the tire changing over with, so Skip got out the air wrench and started the compressor engine while Hermann and Luigi wheeled out the tires. They worked for two hours for they had to be careful not to scratch or mark the magnesium racing wheels; a crack always developed from a scratch or nick. The gas tanks were filled to keep moisture from collecting and would be drained in the morning, and then they put away their tools and left while the last race was in progress.

At the motel Skip bathed and changed clothes. Someone knocked on his door and he opened it. Otto and his mother and Anne Bechel laughed and came in. "Well for gosh sakes," Skip said. "I'll be darned!"

"You can't say that he's speechless," Otto said. "We decided to come on down and see the races tomorrow.

We're staying in a motel in Salinas; this place was all filled up."

"We hoped to catch you and have dinner together, Skip," his mother said. "You haven't eaten yet?"

"No, and I'm glad I don't have to eat alone."

"Where's Sandy and Les?" Otto said.

"They quit. A long story. I'll tell you over the salad." He looked at Anne and smiled. "Have you heard any more about Larry?"

"He called once. We talked awhile. He has to appear next Thursday, and I guess he's a little worried."

"Jim Vale is going to let him start to work on Monday," Skip told her.

Otto whistled softly. "Now there's a change of heart if I ever saw one." Then he laughed. "We passed a nice place on the way in, if you can stand to ride in a Volkswagen after playing with all those expensive cars."

"I'd ride in a nose cone if you wanted, Pop."

They went out and crowded into the Volkswagen. Otto turned north on the highway, going a mile before pulling into a large parking lot by a steak house. Inside, colored lights played a pattern on the ceiling, there was a fire in the big fireplace, and the place was full of the aroma of steaks cooking over charcoal, mixed with the smell of spices and garlic bread.

They ordered, and Otto Hansen asked, "If Sandy and Les aren't driving, who is?"

Skip told him as much as he knew. "Of course I've got Jim Vale's version of it and that's that Les and Sandy are a couple of ingrates for not stepping aside this time while someone else drove. I don't know what's right and what's wrong; it's not for me to decide those things, but I can't blame them for walking out." He laughed and shook his head. "You'd think Vale knew both of them better than that."

"Sometimes a man thinks so hard about winning something that he just doesn't consider anything else," Otto said. "Who's managing the pits with Les gone?"

"I am. I get along with Hermann because I can rattle off German as fast as he can. Luigi goes by hand motions. I don't think he'll ever learn English. He's a real smash around the shop; he talks with his hands and eyes and when he gets mad he sits in the middle of the floor and bangs a hammer. But he's kind of a genius and nobody cares how temperamental he gets." Then he stopped a moment and bunched his eyebrows. "Now that's funny, isn't it? I mean, we never get sore at Luigi for flying off the handle, but when Jim Vale goes on a tear, everybody gets shook up about it."

"Don't you know the answer?" Otto said.

"Am I supposed to?" Skip asked.

"I think you've already told us the answer," his mother said. "Luigi is kind of a genius. When he loses his temper it isn't really to get his own way, is it now?"

"Why, I guess it isn't. But I never thought of it that way. Luigi gets mad at the world and the sun. I don't think the things we do ever bother him. He's really a nice guy."

"People are complicated," Otto said, "and that's what makes them worth knowing."

"I could do with a lot less of it," Skip said dryly. "I

just hope tomorrow is a good day and all the cars hold together."

"And if they don't?" Anne asked.

Skip shrugged. "Well, three guesses as to who Jim Vale will blame for it."

Chapter 5

VIEW FROM THE PIT

Aₗₜₕₒᵤ𝒼ₕ sᴋɪᴘ got to bed early, he did not sleep
well because he worried about the cars. When he finally
did sleep he dreamed that engines blew up and gear boxes
failed and that he had turned all thumbs when he tried
to make repairs.

Just before dawn he woke from a particularly bad
dream and decided to get up. Hermann and Luigi were
still sleeping, so Skip took the motorcycle and rode into
town where he found an all night restaurant open. He sat
down, ordered bacon and eggs and fretted until the waitress brought them.

After he ate he went out to the course. He was the
first one there, and the dawn was just graying the tops of
the hills. He started the generator for lights, and went
about the business of warming the cars, taking them out
on the course one by one, motoring easily because the
blacktop was slick and he had no intention of going off
the road and bending one of the cars.

When Hermann and Luigi arrived, they drained the

gasoline tanks, checked the tires and oil and took off the engine cowlings for a minute inspection to make sure that nothing was coming adrift. It was during this inspection that Skip noticed the familiar cracks in the fire wall where the throttles connected. How many laps the cars would travel before the throttles broke was anyone's guess, but they would break; Skip was certain of that.

He didn't have Les Malloy to argue with this time, so he wrote out what he wanted, gave the paper to Hermann and sent him into town with it. There was some doubt in Skip's mind that the auto parts houses would be open, but he was hoping that some of the body shops would be.

As nine o'clock approached, the drivers came out to practice in their cars, and when Hermann returned it was almost eleven-thirty. The three cars were not going as fast as they had been; Luigi was keeping track with the stop watches, but Skip could tell by the exhaust noise that the engines were just not turning up the revs.

Then Ginther came in and complained of lost power; he got out of the car, walked over to the van, and helped himself to the coffee thermos. Skip and Hermann took off the cowling and while Hermann removed the throttle assembly, Skip got some aluminum from the van and cut a large fishplate to be mounted on the fire wall.

Hill and Gurney came in, crabbing about lost power; Skip told them he'd take care of it and went on working. In an hour he had the whole bell crank glued to the fire wall with epoxy resin and a patch over the torn part.

There wasn't time to do a clean, professional job, and Skip winced when he looked at the smears of resin, the gobs of it holding the bracket in place. It was almost noon and there was very little time left for practice and time trials for grid position. He wanted the epoxy to dry properly, so he kept the cars in the pits, which irritated the drivers.

Time trials began and still Skip held the cars in the pits until the last twenty minutes. Then he had no choice but to let them go. Three fuming drivers stormed out onto the course, determined to knock seconds off the old record.

Jim Vale, arriving late, came into the pits and wanted to know why the devil his boys hadn't qualified yet. Hermann shrugged and Luigi pretended that he didn't understand, but he did, perfectly, and Skip patiently explained about the throttle developing the usual cracks on the fire wall.

This had no soothing effect on Vale; he had someone to blame and ranted a bit and again left Skip with the responsibility.

Gurney was the fastest driver; he left a time that no one could seem to break, and when trials ended, Ginther and Gurney sat in the first row of the grid, with Hill two rows back; he claimed to be still a little down on power.

Skip jerked off the cowling and found that the resin hadn't hardened enough to hold on the fire wall, and there was some doubt in his mind if it would harden in time for the race, scheduled for three o'clock. If it didn't it wouldn't be because he didn't try. He spent an hour cleaning off the old resin, making a new patch and putting it back together again.

When it came time to line up the cars for the main event, Skip had the two cars for Ginther and Gurney pushed out and placed, and held off on the other car as long as he could to give the patch as much time as possible to dry.

Then the announcer cleared the grid, engines were started, the starter made his run down to see that every driver was ready to go, the flag fell, and the cars roared away up the hill. It was an exciting thing, all that noise, fumes, and rushing cars, but somehow it made Skip feel tired. He sat down and worried some more.

Hermann and Luigi worked the stop watches and the blackboards to signal the drivers; this was no concern of Skip's, so he got some pop out of the cooler and leaned against the fender of the pickup, trying to think of something pleasant.

He could hear the loud speakers set about the course blaring, echoing each other; all the announcers on the turns seemed very excited and it was difficult to understand what they were saying. But every minute and seventeen seconds a gaggle of cars burst past with fury and noise, zooming up the hill and away.

He felt tired, more drained and exhausted then ever before. Gurney was leading still, and the announcer was shouting his enthusiasm and making a running commentary on the race. Skip turned him off and went over to help Hermann load the worn tires into the van.

There would be no pit stops for the drivers unless they ran into trouble, and if that happened, it would probably mean that the car was scratched, for ten minutes lost could not be regained in a race two hundred miles long.

Gurney was not leading by such a margin that he could relax, for a little Scotsman in a factory Lotus was yapping at his heels and this gave the announcers an exciting topic of conversation.

Jim Vale came into the pits; he wore a large smile and he put his arm around Skip's shoulders, speaking loudly to be heard above the din of sports car racing. "I spoke harshly to you awhile back, boy. You know I'm sorry, that I didn't mean it."

Skip looked at him for a moment, and then said, "It's all right; I've forgotten all about it." This pleased Vale. When he left, Skip wondered why he had said that. Actually he found Vale difficult to understand, difficult to get along with, but you just didn't tell the boss that, not if you wanted to keep your job.

Skip left the pits and climbed to the crown of the hill overlooking the start-finish line; he found his folks and Anne Bechel there and he squatted beside them. Otto said, "We're going back as soon as the race is over. Are you bringing the van?"

Skip nodded. "Anne, do you want to ride back with me?"

"How late will we get in?"

He made some mental calculations. "Eleven, I guess."

She shook her head regretfully. "I'd like to, but I'd better not. Sorry."

"So am I," he said and turned his attention briefly to the race; it droned on, the drivers pretty well set in their position. Then he got up, saying, "I've got to get back. If a car pulled in and I wasn't there, Mr. Vale would hit the roof."

He left them and went back to the pits in order to straighten the gasoline cans in the van, roll the air hose, and put everything in its place. Luigi came over and helped him stack the tires; they loaded the work-horse into the van then went to the pit wall and watched the race.

Skip kept looking toward the knoll where his parents and Anne Bechel watched but he couldn't see them at all. All this work sure took the fun out of a race weekend; if he hadn't had to stay in the pits he could have eaten hot dogs, and drunk bottled pop with Anne and his parents.

Skip would have liked to have brought his family into the pits, but the organizers charged a good bit of money for pit passes. Knowing Otto's deep-rooted sense of thrift, Skip realized that the idea was impractical.

So he felt left out and knew that it was unreasonable but he couldn't help it. He tried to talk himself out of it by admitting that it was childish.

By the time the race ended, nine cars had dropped out with mechanical trouble, but none of them belonged to Jim Vale. None of the Vale cars won either. Jimmy Clark in a factory Lotus won, and Gurney had to content himself with second place. The other two Vale cars placed fourth and fifth and Skip Hudson really didn't care much by then.

Hermann and Luigi helped him load the cars; they cleaned up the pit area and closed the van. By that time the stream of spectators' cars had dwindled to nothing, the sun was down, and a deep chill settled.

Hermann and Luigi wanted to take the pickup back so Skip took the Diesel van, grinding his way to the access roads in first gear. When he reached town he turned north on the highway and rolled at a steady fifty-five until he saw a diner ahead and pulled in, letting the engine idle while he ate.

The nervous tension he had felt over the weekend was beginning to wear on him and he felt incredibly tired, but the hot roast beef sandwich and three cups of coffee put some go back into him. He felt better when he pulled into traffic and started north again.

He had a four hour drive ahead of him and he hoped the traffic on the Oakland freeway would be light.

It wasn't, but it moved along at a reasonable rate and there were no accidents to cause a four-mile jam up. He finally pulled into the parking area behind Vale's place, locked the truck, got into his Healey and drove home.

Otto and his mother were still up, although it was after eleven, but he was too tired to talk; he took a shower and went to bed and fell immediately to sleep.

Skip's alarm jolted him awake and the aroma of breakfast cooking got him out of bed. After dressing, he went into the kitchen and sat across from Otto, who was reading the morning paper.

Otto put the paper down and said, "What's Vale trying to do, prove he can go faster than the factory cars?" He laughed and shook his head. "Some men just have to win all the time. I've got nothing against winning, but it tends to make an unhappy man unhappier." He sliced his ham and ate. "Larry starts to work today, huh? Try to keep him out of trouble."

"Just how far do I have to go for this guy, Pop?"

"As far as your conscience says," Otto advised. "You know. I don't have to tell you."

"It can get to be a lot of bother," Skip said.

He finished his breakfast, gave his mother a hug, and went out and got into his car. He was a few minutes early when he pulled behind Vale's place, but Vale was there and the back door was unlocked. George Ryder, who was service manager in the general maintenance shop, waved from his glassed in office.

It seemed strange to Skip to come in and not find Les Malloy there. The other mechanics in the competition department arrived and stood around after punching in; no one started to work because there was no one to tell them what needed to be done. Most of them knew but no one wanted to assume the authority.

Paul Lavery, a lath-thin man in his mid-thirties, said, "Are we going to stand here all day or what?"

Another said, "Why don't you go ask Vale?"

"You ask him," Lavery said.

The man shook his head. "Not me."

"I'll go ask him," Skip said and walked through the corridor past parts and on to the front offices. Vale's door was partially open and he could hear Vale talking to someone; Skip knocked, pushed the door open, then stepped inside. Larry Wise was sitting across from Vale, who was tilted back in his chair, annoyed at the interruption.

"Well?" Vale asked.

"The men are ready to go to work, Mr. Vale. Who's in charge of the department?"

"Don't tell me you can't find something to do," Vale snapped.

"Yes, sir, there's plenty to do, but I don't think they want to just go ahead without work orders and a supervisor."

"Then you go back there and get them started."

Skip shook his head. "That wouldn't be right because I don't know enough about it."

"Look, I've been trying to get Les Malloy on the phone, so go on back there and keep your shirt on." He waved his hand impatiently. "And take this fella with you."

"You mean, Larry, sir?"

"YesImeanLarry!"

Skip made a motion with his head. Larry Wise went out ahead of him and they walked back to the shop together. The men stood around Les Malloy's office, waiting. Skip said, "He's trying to get ahold of Les. He just wants us to do something."

"Now that's what I call definite," Paul Lavery admitted. He looked around from one to the other. "Is it all right with you if I go through Les' work orders? I mean, we ought to get busy. It bothers me, just standing around."

They nodded and murmured their agreement and Paul Lavery went into Malloy's office, checked the rack of work orders, and began handing them out. When he came to Skip, he looked at Larry and said, "Is he working with you?"

"Yes," Skip said and took the work order. He walked over to his workbench and studied it carefully. Larry hung over his shoulder. "Stop breathing down my neck," Skip said matter-of-factly. He wrote down a number on a piece of paper and handed it to Larry. "Around the east side of the building there are some cars parked. This is a new Lotus Elite; that's the chassis number. Drive it in here because we have to give it the Vale go-treatment for racing." He smiled. "Try not to crash in flames, huh?"

For a second Larry looked like he was going to take it wrong, then he laughed and trotted out.

They spent the morning getting the car up on a chassis stand and removing the engine; when this was bolted to the stand, Vale came out into the shop, whistled, and they all stopped work and went over to see what the news was.

"Who handed out the work orders?" Vale asked.

Lavery held up his hand, but didn't say anything.

"Who told you to do that?" Vale wanted to know.

"Nobody, but it was better than standing around twiddling our thumbs," Lavery said.

"Neither Malloy nor Sanderson are coming back," Vale said, his manner blunt. "Paul, you're the foreman, if you want the job. And the pay that goes with it."

"I'll take it," Lavery said, "because I look simply divine in a white shop coat."

The men laughed but Vale didn't. "We've got a lot of work to do on some of these cars, and since Skip's been working with Malloy and Sanderson, I'm putting him in charge of the weekend testing. He can use Hermann and Luigi and—"

"Mr. Vale, I don't know enough about—"

Vale stared at him and Skip closed his mouth. "You can drive and you can write, and what you can't fix at the course you can bring back here for someone to fix. Is that spelled out clear enough?" Skip nodded and Vale went on. "In a week or ten days I'll be lining up some drivers. It wasn't my intention to mention this, but in the spring we're taking a team to Europe." This created a mild buzz and he waited for it to die down. "We're going to enter a team of Lotus Elites at LeMans, France. It would be nice to take the team prize away from the factory."

"Like borrowing money from Fort Knox," Lavery said dryly.

"You're a real comic," Vale said. "Any questions? The department's taken a shaking, but we'll live through it."

"Just a minute," Paul Lavery said. "Mr. Vale, we all know what happened to Sanderson and Malloy. We wouldn't want it to happen to us. A trip to Europe takes some family planning and we wouldn't want to make any disappointing last minute changes."

Vale stared at him. "Just what do you think happened to Malloy and Sanderson?"

"You sold 'em out for three other hot-shoes," Lavery said.

Color came into Vale's face and he glared at Skip Hudson. "You just couldn't keep your mouth shut, could you?"

"He didn't say anything," one man snapped. "He didn't have to. Malloy called me that night and told me he was through."

"When a man works for me, I demand his loyalty," Vale said flatly. "And I get it."

"But what does *he* get?" Lavery asked. "Don't kid yourself, Jim. We all like it here. Good pay, good shop, and the best equipment, but it's not the first job we've had and it likely won't be the last. Kind of keep that in mind, huh?"

Chapter 6

LARRY LEARNS THE HARD WAY

Three days before Larry Wise had to appear in court, he received a notice that the hearing had been set off a month. The judge had to have abdominal surgery and the other calendars were too full to permit a shifting to another judge. This suited Larry just fine.

On the job, he was somewhat of a problem. He wasn't lazy, but he was careless and always in a hurry. He made many mistakes which Skip would catch, warn him, and hope that it would do some good.

Paul Lavery twice came close to firing Larry, but held back because Skip was trying hard to get Larry to do more and talk less.

Larry was cursed by a big mouth, and it got him into trouble. He just could not understand that it was not his place to go into the parts rooms and over to the mainte-nance section, borrow tools, and not take them back. And it seemed that he could just never bring himself to say that he was wrong, or sorry for anything. Skip got tired of making excuses for him, tired of holding his temper.

They had been changing the rear-end ratios in one of Cooper racing cars, a tedious job with a lot of disassembly, and the floor was greasy when it came time to clean up for the night. Skip was cleaning tools and he told Larry to mop up the floor. Skip thought nothing more about it until Paul Lavery came over to the bench and said, "I hope you're going to clean up that mess before you leave."

"What me—" Skip began, and then saw that the floor hadn't been touched. "Where's Larry?"

"Taking a shower," Lavery said. "Did you tell him to—" His lips pulled into a hard, flat line. "All right, I've had him right up to here." He laid a finger across his eyebrows and started to turn.

Skip grabbed his arm. "I got him this job. Let me handle it." He put down the tools he had been cleaning and walked across the shop to the washroom. Three men came out, waved and left; there was no one in the place now except Lavery.

Larry was out of the shower and dressing; he looked up when Skip came in the washroom and grinned.

"I thought I told you to clean up that floor," Skip said.

"Man, it'll wait until morning." He bent over to tie his shoes and Skip's temper snapped. He grabbed Larry by his thick hair, swung him like a ball on a string and bounced him against the metal lockers.

Larry lost his balance, fell to his hands and knees, and stayed there, looking up at Skip Hudson. "I guess you started something, man."

"No, *you* did," Skip told him.

Paul Lavery came in and stood by the door; he looked

from one to the other and said, "Handle this to suit yourself, Skip. Nobody will bother you."

"I'm sure going at it the wrong way," Skip admitted. "I was going to solve it by fighting."

"Yeah, that's the wrong way," Lavery said. He looked at Larry Wise. "Didn't he tell you to do something? Then you get out there and get it done. When someone tells you to do something in this shop, you jump, see? And if that doesn't suit you, you can leave right now. There are no more chances around here for you, friend. This is your last one. So what's it going to be?"

Larry got up and dusted off his knees. "It didn't seem important to me to—"

"Listen, it's not for you to decide. *We* decide. You *do*. Get it?"

"Yeah, I get it."

"Then act like it. Now get going because I want to get home."

Larry slipped into his coveralls, went out, and got a bucket of solvent and a mop. Lavery and Skip watched a moment; then Lavery said, "I'm going to cut out. Lock the side door, huh?" He gave Skip a playful slap on the head and left. Skip walked over to where Larry was working. Without pausing with the mopping, Larry said, "You could give me a hand."

"I did my job. Now you do yours. What do you expect people to do, pick up after you? Can't you get smart? Nobody owes you anything at all."

"I never thought you'd get hard nosed about this, Skip. I thought you were my friend."

"Just what does that mean to you? Does that mean I

cover for you, wait on you, alibi for you? Lavery wasn't kidding. You get on the dime right now or you're fired. This job isn't any favor to you. You earn your pay and you keep you fat mouth shut."

Larry glared and went into one of his sulks, but he cleaned the floor thoroughly and went out. Skip locked up and Larry started toward the road.

"You want a ride?" Skip asked.

"I'd rather walk!"

"Suit yourself," Skip said and got into his car. He started it, let it warm for a moment, then pulled out. Larry was holding up his thumb but his chance of getting someone to stop along Willow Pass was pretty remote; people were going home and they didn't want to pick up anyone.

Skip stopped the car and said, "Now you gave me a stupid answer a minute ago. Do you still want to stick by it?"

Larry looked at him, then shook his head and got into the car. As Skip started up, Larry said, "What's the matter with me? Can't I do anything right?"

"You want the truth?" He looked at Larry. "The trouble is, you can't do *anything*, right or wrong. Everybody ought to have something to be proud of, but you don't have anything. I'd get something if I were you and I wouldn't waste any time about it."

"How do you know that's so?"

"I'm no smarter than you," Skip said. "And for every mistake you can make, I can make two. This isn't a contest we're in, Larry. It's a tough world and we've got to get along in it." He fell silent for a moment. "It seems to me you try pretty hard to goof. If you tried as hard to do a good job, you'd feel a lot better about it. There's two ways to get noticed. Doing right is a lot slower, but it's more satisfying."

"My old man says I'll never amount to anything."

"Then don't listen to him."

"How can I help it? He keeps yappin' all the time."

Skip laughed. "Then make him out a liar. Then you can laugh at him and throw it up to him that he was wrong." It was a poor way to go about the problem, Skip knew, but he felt that he had to reach Larry someway.

Larry smiled and rubbed his hands together. "Boy, wouldn't I like to do that! Why not? Yeah! Why not?" He settled down in the seat, his mood completely changed. Skip said nothing more, not even when he let Larry out in front of his house.

And then he forgot about it because he took Anne Bechel to the movies. Afterward they sat up with her folks eating popcorn and watching a funny English movie on television.

It was a quarter to one when Skip got home. The house was dark, so he went to bed and the next morning he didn't even remember the incident.

As soon as Skip got to work, Paul Lavery called him over. "Vale wants the team cars taken to Fawndale this weekend. Hermann and Luigi will go with you." He reached over and pulled out some sheets of paper from a drawer. "Malloy set this up some time ago so I guess the old man's had this cooking. Twenty-four hours is a long time, Skip, and the pit stops have to be fast and no goofing anywhere. It'll mean drill and more drill until you can gas the cars, change the tires and driver in a matter of thirty seconds. So you'd better pick another man and get going on it." He handed the papers to Skip. "These are the race regulations; it'll take some studying before you understand them. You can set up your own training schedules. I don't know who's going to be driving, but that's not our worry. Right?"

"You are so right," Skip said and went over to his workbench.

Vale had provided four Elite coupes for the team cars, one to be the work horse; they were all white with racing stripes running darkly from radiator opening to blunt tail. The engines had all been worked over carefully, modified considerably, with only the limits of the displacement intact.

Skip spent most of the morning figuring out what equipment they would want to take along with them on Saturday, and he gave the list to Larry to be loaded into the van; Skip half expected this to be fouled up and when he checked later, he found that it had been done exactly as he had specified. All the spare tires and wheels were racked, and the tools were in the proper drawers. Larry had even swept out the van.

Friday afternoon the cars were loaded and the van locked and parked in back. Hermann and Luigi would take the pickup and Skip told Larry to meet him in front of his house at a quarter after six.

One of the office girls came back and gave Lavery their pay checks and for the first time since he had started, Larry did not rush over, first in line. This rather surprised Lavery, but he said nothing about it and neither did Skip.

"A couple more of those and you can get your pickup fixed," Skip said, just making conversation.

"I junked it for forty dollars," Larry said, folding the check. "I've been paying the old man twenty bucks a week and banking the rest. It's pretty good, paying him twenty bucks a week. At least he's stopped calling me a chow-hound all the time." He grinned. "My back was getting sore, with him always on it. But with a job, he can't say much. I work just as steadily as he does."

"You're running on the wrong track," Skip said.

"What's that mean?"

"Forget it. See you tomorrow morning and don't be late."

When the alarm clock rang, Skip moaned and fumbled for it; but he got up as soon as he turned it off, dressed, went into the kitchen and put on the coffee pot. His mother came in a few minutes later, a robe belted about her.

"Are you going to work every weekend?"

"Sure looks like it," he said and switched on the gas range.

"I'll fix your breakfast," she said, and he busied himself making a lunch. "Otto told me to ask you if it would be all right if he went along one of these times."

"Sure," Skip said. "He can come along today if he likes. But it's a poor hour for a working man to get up unless he's going fishing." He got up, went into the back bedroom, and gave Otto a gentle shake, waking him. "Want to come along today, Pop?"

"Sure," Otto said and got out of bed, yawning and

rubbing his thinning hair. Skip went into the kitchen and Otto came out a few minutes later; it was still dark outside, but growing light. "Thank God you get overtime for this," he said and laughed. "I always said that these sportsmen racing drivers were balmy to do this for fun."

"I sure wouldn't do it," Skip admitted. "I like my sleep. Besides, I know what it costs. Do you know that some of these men pay six hundred dollars a race just to keep their cars winning?"

If a man has a lot of money," Otto said, "six hundred dollars is not much."

"It sure would be if he gave that much to the Community Chest," Skip said.

Otto Hansen's head came up quickly and his voice turned firm. "Now wait a minute. Let's not sit there and throw blanket judgments around. You don't know anything about what a man does with his money, so let's watch it, huh?"

Embarrassment colored Skip's face. "Gosh, Pop, I just wasn't thinking."

Otto tapped him on the forehead with his finger. "Then think. It won't hurt you." He poured some coffee, added sugar, and sat with his hands around the cup. "Have you decided whether or not you're going to stick with Vale?" Skip shrugged slightly. "What I mean is, have you given up any idea of going on to college?"

"I don't know," Skip said. "Even if a man goes to college, isn't a job what he's really after? Sooner or later we all settle on a trade and that's that. I don't know if college and a degree are so important."

"A degree makes the difference between who dirties the test tubes and who washes them," Otto said.

"That's kind of simplifying it, isn't it, Pop?"

"Sure, but we ought to get to the basic truth. Right now Vale's looks good. It'll look good ten years from now, a nice pay check every week, but when you get to be thirty you'll realize that you'll never be any better, or go any higher, and then you'll understand what you passed up. Am I reaching you, Skip?"

"Loud and clear." He got up and looked at his wristwatch. "Time to go."

It was sprinkling outside, so Skip took along his raincoat. Otto came out and opened the garage door and backed out the Volkswagen; they got in and drove over to pick up Larry Wise, who was standing on the curb in front of his house, shoulders hunched against the chill drizzle.

Larry got into the back seat and rubbed his hands together. "Man, don't you call these things off on account of rain?"

"They race in the rain," Skip said. "It's good practice."

"Getting wet?" Larry asked and laughed. He shook out a cigarette and lit it.

Otto parked the VW in back of Vale's and Skip went over to the Diesel rig, got it started, and fast idled it to warm it up. He made a last minute check to see if he'd forgotten anything, decided he hadn't, and the others got in the huge cab and crowded around the heater while he pulled slowly onto the highway.

They had gone a few miles before Larry said, "Skip,

you don't suppose Vale's got it in mind to let you drive for him, do you?"

Skip shook his head. "He wouldn't offer it and I wouldn't take it. He let Sanderson and Malloy go and they were better drivers than I'd ever be. No, he just wants me to run some time on the cars, that's all."

"Well, Malloy and Sanderson didn't go broke working for Vale," Larry said, as a reminder. "If he ever offered me a chance, I'd take it."

When Skip turned in at the spectator's gate, he found it unlocked, and drove in. Then he saw Sanderson's car near the pits, and Malloy's three-year-old Jaguar sedan. There was a van belonging to a San Francisco-based racing team parked along the pit wall and two special racing Jaguar coupes were on the course, motoring rapidly, sending up a rooster-tail of water as they plunged down the straight and on into the first turn.

Skip parked Vale's van; Hermann and Luigi were waiting in the pickup, and they got out and helped him unload the work horse Lotus coupe.

Hermann said, "Those British Motor Car people go *schnell.*" He nodded toward the two Jaguars on the course.

"Isn't that Vale's main competition?"

Hermann shrugged. "He thinks he can beat anybody."

The Jaguars finally had enough and came in, then Skip stared in surprise as Sanderson and Les Malloy climbed out. They came over, shaking hands with Skip, who then introduced them to Otto Hansen.

"Are you driving for British Cars now?" Skip asked.

"Why not?" Malloy asked. "Heard you did very zippy

at Laguna Seca. Hated to walk off like that old boy, but what does a man do? Pride, you know."

"Sure, I know. I can understand that, Les." He smiled. "Say, if you go out again, how about me following you around? Maybe I can watch and learn something."

Chapter 7

CRACK-UP AT THE TRACK

SKIP knew that one thing a racing driver did not do was to give away time to another driver, not even a tenth of a second because it all added up and in the end determined who would win a race and who would lose.

The LeMans start was world famous, with the cars parked parallel on one side of the course with the drivers on the mark on the other side. At the starting gun, they would scoot for their cars, jump in, start, and get away in a thundering pack. Precious time could be lost there, fumbling for a seatbelt or shoulder harness, fighting a balky gearbox, or finding an engine difficult to start when hot.

Even the pit stops were crucial, for the driver had to be out of the car and on the pit wall before the mechanics were allowed to touch the car, and then only a certain number could work on the car.

It was Skip's job, through testing and trial and error, to eliminate as many flaws as possible in the car and procedure. And right away he found that the seatbelt harness was installed wrong because when getting in, the driver would invariably sit on the buckle, thereby wasting time unsnarling it.

The belts would have to be reversed; he made a note to do that in the shop. There were other things needed, like the seat adjustment; the deep buckets were hard to get into unless the seat was all the way back, and then the driver had to waste time fooling with it to get it right. He made a note of that and decided to figure out some quick, preset adjusting device.

Hermann and Larry were practicing wheel-changing while Luigi manned the quick-lift jack, and Otto, to keep busy, was checking them with a stop watch and keeping a record of the times, trying to get the lost motion worked out of their job.

Sanderson and Malloy, in the pits farther down, started up and pulled out onto the course with the Jaguars. Skip got a helmet and got into one of the Elite coupes. He started the engine and added just enough throttle to keep it running smoothly; all the engines had been modified until they developed some cranky qualities but put out a high horsepower rating. When the engine was hot, he got out, opened the hood and quickly changed sparkplugs, installing a colder, racing plug.

Sanderson and Malloy were circulating at speed and Skip pulled out onto the wet course, accelerating hard down the pit straight. He went around a few times, getting the feel of the car in the rain, and kept increasing his speed.

Malloy was somewhere behind him, but he could see Sanderson ahead, and in five laps Skip had gained slightly on him; Sanderson's car, with all that power, was sliding about a bit too much in the back S's.

For ten laps they stayed well together and when they came out of the tight hairpin turn leading onto the mile long straight, Skip would drive in Sanderson's wheel spray and slip-stream him all the way down, reaching speeds of 145 miles an hour, the back suction of the Jaguar pulling the smaller, lighter Lotus along.

Skip braked quickly and hard for the fast banked turn and Sanderson's brake lights went on briefly, then went out, and he entered the corner way too fast, the rear of the car sliding first. Then Sanderson's car spun four times, went over the banked portion of the corner, flipped in the air, hit, bounced, flipped again, and Skip zoomed past, unable to get on the brakes in the corner. He slid the car a little, letting that slow him, and he thought of stopping and turning back but he knew that the quickest way to the pits was on around the course and standing on it all the way.

When Skip came out of the hairpin and braked for the pits, the others were already climbing into the pickup; he stopped and Otto jerked open the passenger door, folded himself inside, and Skip left with spinning wheels, leaving the pickup and the others behind.

Even with a standing start, the Lotus was cracking a hundred miles an hour when Skip got on the brakes hard and entered the turn, slowing way down. He could see the marks made by Sanderson's tires where he went over and he slid the small car to a stop there, grabbed the fire extinguisher and jumped out, sliding in the mud down the short embankment to the Jaguar, on its side, one wheel still turning.

Hermann came screeching up in the pickup, boldly drove down the ten-foot incline, and parked by the wrecked Jaguar. Skip was yanking at the door and making little headway at it until Luigi inserted a steel bar, applied pressure and sprung the lock.

Otto fastened a tow cable to the car and Hermann looped it over the trailer hitch of the pickup; he pulled forward and banged the Jaguar back on its wheels. Sanderson was unconscious and bleeding from a few head and facial cuts but Skip paid little attention to that. The damage had pinned his right leg badly and Skip knew they'd have to cut part of the car away to get him out.

Les Malloy arrived alone. His crew had left to get sandwiches and he went back to the Vale pits with Hermann to get the welding torch and more tools. Otto pushed Luigi aside and looked closely at the damage. Then he said, "Let's get the damaged cowling off so we can see what's holding him in there."

Skip helped him; they unfastened the nose piece but had to wrench it heavily to break it free. The front motor mounts had let go, letting the engine and gearbox shift to the left and pin Sanderson's leg.

Hermann came back with the pickup and Otto got a hydraulic jack and a block of wood and bent down, working the handle, slowly forcing the engine back toward the centerline. Sanderson groaned and Otto, without looking up, said, "Lift him out of there, but be careful. His leg's surely broken."

He kept pressure on the jack while Hermann, with a

long pry bar, forced over the brake pedal and freed Sanderson's leg. Larry spread a canvas on the ground where they laid Sanderson out and Skip saw that his leg was badly mangled; the coveralls were torn and bloody.

"I'll go call an ambulance," Malloy said and started up the muddy slope to his car.

"Get a highway patrolman," Skip said. "It'll be quicker because he'll radio in."

Larry got into the pickup and backed it down, close to where Sanderson lay, then stretched another piece of canvas over him to keep off the rain. He then took off his mackinaw and wrapped Sanderson to keep him warm and when he looked at Skip, he said, "Believe it or not, I was a Boy Scout with eighteen merit badges."

"Wouldn't it be better to put him in the seat of the truck and warm him with the heater?" Otto asked.

Larry shook his head. "The less you move him the better it will be. Keep him flat and as dry and warm as possible." He looked at the lean-to formed by the back of the pickup. "Isn't there a first aid kit around here anyplace?" He seemed a little offended. "Fifty thousand dollars worth of machine tools and not one first aid kit?"

"There's one in the cab of the van!" Skip said, remembering. "Right next to the flare box. I'll get it." He clawed up the slope, getting himself muddy, and raced off in the Lotus. A few minutes later he came back with a square metal box and Larry took it and broke open the lead seal.

"A couple of you stand at the other end of this lean-to," Larry said. "Block off as much of it as you can with your legs. Skip, fire up the welding torch and hold it near the other end; we'll get some heat in here." He took the first aid box and crawled into the lean-to with Sanderson and with a pocket knife cut open the leg of his coveralls.

Skip, holding the torch with its big heating tip roaring, made a face when he saw Sanderson's leg. But it didn't seem to bother Larry. He broke a sulfa pack and liberally dusted the compound fracture.

Then he took out a morphine vial, broke off the slender glass end and jabbed it into Sanderson's arm. Larry broke open some thick bandage packs and laid them over the injury and after this was done, he got out the smelling salts and waved it under Sanderson's nose, making him cough and open his eyes.

Somewhere down the highway a siren wailed like a lonesome dog, drawing nearer. Larry smiled and said, "The Marines are coming, dad." He glanced at the rain-darkened canvas lean-to. "Not fancy, but we call it home." Sanderson tried to move but Larry quickly pressed him motionless. "No foot racing, pops. Doctor Wise's orders. OK?"

"OK," Sanderson said softly.

The siren wailed closer, then shut down quickly, and a burly highway patrolman jumped out of his car; there was another man with him, carrying a familiar bag.

"You got here in a hurry," Skip said.

"Excuse me," the doctor said, kneeling in the mud.

Les Malloy came back and parked and the doctor was making his examination. He saw the open first aid kit and said, "Who's been—"

"I did," Larry said. "I've already given him a jolt of morphine to kill the pain. Is there an ambulance on the way?"

"Yes," the policeman said. "How is he, doc?"

"He's as comfortable as can be expected. There's nothing more I can do at the moment. He's got shelter and heat, he's in no particular pain, and the likelihood of infection in the wound has been reduced." He crawled out and glanced briefly at his ruined suit. "I'll go in with the ambulance though."

The patrolman looked around. "Don't you people have a doctor or any fire fighting equipment out here when you're testing cars? Haven't you ever heard of safety? This man could have been killed." He turned to his patrol car. "I'll go up to the gate and make sure the ambulance gets here all right."

After he pulled away, the doctor looked down at Sanderson. "Feeling any pain?"

"No. Just cold and jumpy, doc."

"Shock," the doctor said. "We'll have you in a hospital before you know it. You've made a mess of that leg but I think we can straighten it out." He walked over and looked at the badly bent Jaguar. "How fast was he going?" he asked Skip.

"About a hundred and twenty."

"That's rapid, isn't it?" The doctor cocked his head to side and they heard another siren drawing closer. A few minutes later the ambulance pulled to a stop at the lip of the turn and the attendants got down.

A stretcher was brought down and Sanderson was gently transferred to it, placed inside, and the ambulance left. Skip said, "I don't know about you people, but I'm for folding it up for today."

No one disagreed, so they loaded the pickup and went

back to the pit area. Malloy's crew came back in his car, wanting to know what the ambulance was doing pulling out of the gate. Skip and Hermann were loading their cars; they pulled out ten minutes later, leaving Malloy and his crew to lock the gate.

It was dark outside. Larry and Skip sat in the hospital waiting room and finally the doctor came out, smiled and said, "No complications, really. We've set the leg, put him in traction, and when the swelling goes down, we'll put a cast on it. Right now he's under sedation and sleeping." He stopped talking as Anne Bechel came hurrying down the hall.

"I was at your house when Otto came home," she said. "Is he hurt badly?"

"No," the doctor said. "You're a good first-aid man, Larry. Now, I have other patients, so if you'll excuse me—"

"Oh, sure," Larry said. "And thanks, doc." He grinned at Skip and Anne Bechel. "I feel like Ben Casey."

"You're out of your head," Skip said. "How did you get over here, Anne?"

"I caught the bus."

They went outside to Skip's car. The rain had stopped but puddles of water stood in the parking lot, bright and shiny under the lights. Anne sat on Larry's lap; the distance was short and she had to hunch over to clear the top.

When they pulled into the garage at Skip's house, Otto switched on the outside lights and came to the back porch. "Is Sandy all right?"

"Yes, he's doing fine, Pop." They walked into the kitchen, which was filled with the aroma of baking. Skip's mother came into the kitchen; he kissed her briefly, then sniffed.

"I know, pie and sandwiches for three," she said. "But you take them into your room on TV trays. Otto has a program he wants to watch without a lot of chatter."

Larry came to attention, clicking his heels, then laughed. Skip got the trays and Anne helped with the sandwiches. Then they took the trays into Skip's room.

"I sure got scared when I saw his leg," Larry admitted. "Things really looked bad but I suppose when it was washed and all—" He looked at the food, then at each of them. "Maybe I ought to shut up while we're eating, huh?"

"You could change the subject without hurting my feelings," Anne Bechel said.

"Larry," Skip said, "you really came through out there. I'm going to make sure Jim Vale knows about it too."

"I don't care whether he knows it or not."

This surprised Skip and Anne; they looked at each other. Anne said, "How come?"

"He doesn't care about me or anyone else. I know his kind." Larry drank some milk. "He thinks about himself all the time. It would break his mouth to say thanks. I'd rather be in jail than to be like him."

"That's some change of tune for you," Anne said frankly.

"Yeah, it is," Larry admitted. "But I don't think either of you know what it's like to wake up hating yourself every day. It's funny, but I don't do that anymore. Well, not very much anyway. That's good, isn't it?" He laughed self-consciously. "I'll bet one of these days I'll even figure out why I worked so hard being a jerk."

"You sure did put the time in on it," Anne said. "But it's nice to be able to talk to you and not get a smart answer, Larry. People want to get along; it's a natural desire, I guess. I'd rather be liked than disliked; it bothers me when people dislike me. I know it bothered you."

"That's sure true," Skip put in. "I can remember what it was like to do something I was told not to do, and then have to come home and explain the mess.

"It's awful hard to take advice," Anne said, "even when you know it's good. We've just got to do for ourselves, huh?"

"Yeah, and foul it up half of the time," Larry said. "But I didn't foul this up, did I, Skip?"

"Horatio at the bridge," Skip admitted. He held up his empty glass. "Refills?" They wanted more so he went and got a two quart carton from the refrigerator and brought it back, topping their glasses. He sat cross legged on his bed, beside Larry; Anne sat in his study chair.

"This fall I'm going to have enough saved up to go to college," Anne said and they looked at her, surprised that she had been thinking about it. "I'd like to teach school. The fourth grade, maybe."

"Hey, that's great!" Larry said, genuinely excited. "I mean it; it's really great, doing it by yourself."

"Well, we just don't have the money," Anne said. "Oh, Dad would pay for part of it, but I have to supply the rest."

"Lately I've been thinking about going to school," Larry said. "And I'd appreciate it if you didn't laugh. I know I'd study now."

"No one's laughing," Skip said seriously.

"Well, I don't want to be a grease-monkey all my life. And if you don't know anything, that's what you end up being. Otto said so." He seemed embarrassed to have spoken out. "Say—ah—Skip, he's not your real dad, is he?"

"No, my father was killed in Korea."

"You two get along all right? I mean—well, you know what I mean."

Skip put his shoulders against the wall and looked at the ceiling. "It's hard to explain about Otto; he's the best man I ever knew. Never once did he try to crowd in and take my dad's place. He just was himself and I loved him because of that. And a couple of times when he popped me good for something I'd done wrong, I knew he was never mad at me. When a thing was done, it was finished forever and I never heard about it again." Then he laughed. "Otto never put himself in a position where I had to choose between him and my dad. He was always Otto, himself, never once pretending he was anything but himself." He straightened and got up. "You two want me to run you home now or do you want to watch TV awhile?"

"Let's watch TV," Anne said. "And I'll take care of the dishes. Neither of you would ever think of it." She made a face at them and carried the trays into the kitchen.

Chapter 8

"A MECHANIC CAN GO
JUST SO FAR"

SKIP had no idea there would be any trouble over Sanderson's accident until Lavery called to him on the following Monday morning and told him that he was wanted in Jim Vale's office.

When Skip got there he found two men with Vale; they were introduced as the president of the sports car club, which controlled all the amateur racing in the United States, and the club's attorney. Vale was in one of his thunderous moods and his bunched brows reminded Skip of storm clouds forming.

"These gentlemen would like to ask you some questions," Vale said.

"Sure," Skip said and looked at George Willis, the club's attorney.

"I'll try to make this brief," Willis said. "Sanderson says that you were following his car when the accident happened."

"Yes, sir."

"What do you think happened?"

"Well, it looked like he just tapped his brakes once and went on into the turn way too fast. The stop lights came on for an instant, then went out. Then he spun and went over the bank. Actually he spun three times before going over."

"Sanderson says his brakes failed. We've had the car checked and found the hydraulic line to one of the rear wheels ruptured. There were also traces of fluid on the course." He adjusted his glasses. "Mr. Hudson, you were driving a Lotus?"

"Yes, sir."

"And you drive at Fawndale often?"

"Yes, just about every weekend. We do a lot of testing there."

"Doesn't it bother you, driving at speed, with no fire protection or medical facilities?"

Skip shook his head. "Until Sandy went on his head, I never gave it a thought, but now I think it would bother me. By that, I mean that it would be in the back of my mind and I'd be pretty careful. Of course, no one wants to go into the tules, but it can happen when you're going fast and hanging the car out there on the ragged edge." He realized that he was talking a lot and closed his mouth.

Sam Frieden, the club president, said, "We don't have you on our records as holding a competition driver's license."

"No, sir, I don't race. All my driving has been done for Mr. Vale."

Frieden smiled thinly. "Don't you think that's a little

foolish, out there driving fast modified cars, with so little experience?"

His tone rather than the words stung Skip Hudson. "Well now, I don't figure I'm any worse off than some of these boys who come in here, buy a car off the floor, spend nine hundred dollars to prepare it, then take it out to one of your sports car races and wipe it out in the first corner because it's their first novice race. I saw one of those things last year at Stockton where nine cars got bent in the first corner. What do you call that?"

Jim Vale slapped his desk and laughed. Frieden gave George Willis a brief glance and shook his head. "Jim," Willis said, "we don't have any control over Fawndale course, but we strongly suggest that you have available during your testing at least minimum medical facilities and some fire fighting equipment." He adjusted his glasses again. "We are fully aware of the support you've given our activities, fielding both production and modified cars in the races. But we don't want the sport to get a bad name through some unfortunate accident, something more serious than Sanderson's."

"Gentlemen, you're really sticking your nose in and advising me how to run my business and spend my money," Vale said.

"We are," George Willis said, "giving you good advice, and you know it. Jim, the club has supported you at every turn of the road. Let's not have a falling out over this."

"What kind of a falling out?" Vale asked. He looked at Frieden. "Sam, you know that Fawndale is the finest race-course on the West Coast, close to being a true European circuit, up hill and down hill, with grass verges and shade trees. It's a garden spot. Now I've always made this available to the club at no cost to you. What falling out?"

"We would hate to close the course for our drivers," Frieden said softly. "It would hurt us both. When you sponsor your professional events, it would eliminate all the Saturday amateur racing. And when we schedule our regular sports car events, it would eliminate your cars and drivers from our field. Let's not butt heads over this."

"You wouldn't do a dumb thing like barring the course," Vale said. "The best course on the coast?"

"We have to protect our drivers," Willis stated. "Jim, we're not asking for the world. A fire truck on the back of a pickup. You go that far and we'll have our course physicians there, providing they can drive a little in their own cars. Tit for tat, Jim. A fair deal and no hard feelings."

Vale pursed his lips and thought about it, and Skip said, "If there's nothing else you wanted, I've got some work—" Willis nodded and Vale waved his hand idly. Skip stepped outside and closed the door. He would have liked to have stayed and watched Jim Vale back up for a change, but he didn't want to push his luck and come out on the short end of the Vale temper.

As he passed the stockroom, he saw Anne Bechel; she framed the question with her lips: "What happened?" Skip shook his head, made an expressive gesture with his hands, and went on to the shop.

Lavery didn't question him at all, and that afternoon, one of the men from the used car lot came over with a three-quarter ton Chevrolet panel truck and work orders filtered down to convert it into an ambulance and fire-fighting truck.

Larry's day to appear in court came at last, and he and Skip took time off.

Jim Vale was supposed to be there, and Larry's father, the two arresting officers, and the probation officer with his report.

Judge Greenwald was an elderly man, rather stern-faced from his years of responsibilities, but he had kindly brown eyes and a very soft voice.

"This hearing, although official, will be conducted as informally as possible," he said, fingering the sheaf of papers before him. "Larry, it seems that you've had a good deal of difficulty with the authorities with your automobile. Is that correct?"

"Yes, sir."

"Two arrests last year for speeding. Four for double parking, and now this last matter which we're going to take up. You've been busy." He looked at Larry Wise, then glanced up and frowned as Jim Vale came in; his tardiness annoyed the judge but he didn't say anything. "Larry, I'm going to be very frank with you. When I have a boy with your background of vehicle violations behind him, I generally take his license away and make him walk for a year. The slower pace is generally beneficial. However, you misbehaved pretty badly this last time and I've seriously considered remanding you to the custody of the Youth Authority for a few months." He paused and looked around his chambers. "However, your young friend came to see me before my illness and spoke in your behalf and I advised the probation officer to keep a close eye on you. I have his report here." He raised his glance to Jim Vale. "You're Larry Wise's employer?"

"Yes, your Honor."

"And his work is satisfactory?"

Vale pursed his lips. "On a par with a new man."

"That doesn't answer my question."

"Satisfactory," Vale said, nodding. "I've received no report to the contrary and my foreman would have reported it if otherwise."

"Do you intend to keep Larry Wise in your employ?"

"Yes," Jim Vale said.

The judge fingered his gray mustache, and looked at Larry. "The probation officer reports that you've broken with your former friends, Larry. Why is that?"

"The night of the accident they went off and left me. They're no friends of mine."

"Do you get along all right on the job?"

Larry opened his mouth to lie, then said, "I'm learning how, sir. I guess I gave everyone a bad time at first. But I'm trying to shape up, sir."

Judge Greenwald almost smiled. "I'll tell you what I've decided, Larry. You've made some serious mistakes, you've wrecked your car, and came close to seriously hurting yourself, along with your companions. I could suspend your license and give you something on your record, but since you have no car now, I'm going to let you keep your license with the provision that you do not drive a vehicle for one year. If you're caught, you'll go to the Youth Authority. Is that clearly understood?"

Larry swallowed heavily. "Yes, sir."

"In addition, I'm advising the probation officer to look in on you from time to time for that same one year period. If at the end of that time he feels that you've mended some of your thoughtless ways, he can so advise me in his report that we can consider the matter closed." He straightened. "Mr. Vale, I'd like to compliment you on your consideration of this boy and giving him a job."

"It was the least I could do, your Honor."

Greenwald nodded. "Then I think we've settled the matter. Thank you for appearing."

When they went outside, Larry said, "Boy, that's as close as I want to come to jail."

His father, standing nearby lighting a cigar, said, "Haven't I always told you to keep your nose clean? Haven't I said that?"

"You talk so much I don't remember what you say," Larry told him and drew a blunt, offended stare. Then his father turned and walked off and Larry looked after him until he disappeared around the bend of the stairs. "Sometimes I wish he'd stay and fight," he said. "Maybe if we had one good fight we'd get to understand each other."

"If you want to patch it up," Skip said, "you'll have to make the first move. Can't you see that?"

"But why me?"

"Because that's the way it is. There are some things that there just isn't any reason for and maybe that's one of them." He nodded. "Let's get back to the shop. We've only been gone a little more than an hour."

Sandy Sanderson left the hospital after the third week, and the next Saturday his wife drove him to Fawndale and parked the car near the Vale pits. Skip Hudson was on the course in a Lotus Elite. It was raining hard. Puddles dotted the straightaway and he roared through them with great splashes. At the far end his brake lights would glow brightly and briefly and then you could hear him up shifting and down shifting through the back S-curves.

Sanderson got out his stop watch and began timing Skip; he did this for ten laps, then Skip slowed and braked down for the pits and got out of the car, dashing over to the building overhang to get out of the downpour.

Then he saw Sanderson's car and went over, squatting so that he was on an eye level with Sanderson. "Spectating today?" Skip said.

"I've had a watch on you," Sandy said, smiling. "You're circulating pretty regularly out there. In ten laps you didn't vary two-tenths of a second. That's the mark of a good driver, to go like a train and just as regularly."

"The cars are going really well," Skip said. "Have you seen Les?"

"He's doing engineering work now in San Francisco. There's a distributor there who's building some pretty fast cars. A mechanic can go just so far and then you've got to call in the brains and slide-rule boys." He caught a slight change in Skip's expression. "Did I say something wrong?"

"You just described my main trouble," Skip said. "I can tell when something's wrong, say in the handling and suspension of a car, but when it comes to making a change, I'm lost."

"You're a bright kid," Sanderson said. "Why don't you go back to school and learn something? You won't find the answer in Vale's shop. Sure, the answer for some guys, but not for you, Skip. You'll ask too many questions and the answers aren't there." He laughed softly and shook out a cigarette. "I want you to take me seriously now. You do that?"

"Sure, Sandy."

"Spend some time on your rump just thinking about all the things you'd like to know and then ask yourself honestly whether or not you're going to learn them at Jim Vale's place. Or any other place like that. Kid, face it. They can get a lead-foot like me to drive their cars and they can get bright young fellas like you to bolt them together, but it took real brains to design this car." He gave Skip's arm a squeeze. "I've got to get back to town. If you see that Larry, you tell him that I really appreciated it, his dropping in to see me."

"I'll tell him Monday morning," Skip said and stepped back while Sanderson's wife started the car. He watched them drive out and still stood there, water cascading over him.

It wasn't easy to ignore the things Sanderson had said, for somehow Skip felt that Sanderson was relating in part some bitter experience of his own, some chances passed up that he had learned to regret.

And Sanderson was right; Skip did feel tugs of inadequacies. There were things he wanted to do and couldn't because he just didn't have the background for it, that mass of knowledge that stands behind every man who creates.

He'd bought two books on chassis engineering and tried to read them, tried hard to study and understand them, but he didn't get past the tenth page before he became hopelessly bogged down. The writers were assuming that the reader had a background of engineering and talked in an engineer's language, mathematics and graphs. It just left Skip Hudson on the curb.

Working at Vale's place had pointed out what he lacked. He was a careful worker, precise, and getting on there was simply a matter of becoming familiar with the cars and engines; they offered little that was new in theory or principle. The things he wanted to learn couldn't be learned there, and like Sanderson had said, probably in no shop.

A man had to go back to the classroom, to the books, and in time he might know enough to do the things his mind kept prodding him to do.

Hermann, over by the course, yelled at him, and Skip realized that he had been standing there, doping off; he felt a little foolish as he trotted back.

"You going to drive more today?" Hermann asked.

"No," Skip said. "Let's put the cars in the garage and come back in the morning, if the sun's shining." He looked at the dull, lead-colored sky. "If it's raining I'm going to sleep in."

"You think Vale will like that?"

"You know, Hermann, I don't really care."

Chapter 9

THE PROS ARE SHOWN UP

Larry wise got a pay raise in December because Paul Lavery liked the way he was shaping up and put in a recommendation to accounting. It was okayed by Jim Vale, who took his foreman's word in these matters.

Since the hearing, Larry had been riding to and from work with Skip Hudson and it got to be a thing, the two of them together. Sometimes Anne would join them and they'd take Otto's VW and go to the movies.

Larry understood that Anne was sort of Skip's girl although they had nothing settled, like going steady; they spent time together because they got along and because they worked at the same place. Larry Wise thought that he was lucky to have such friends.

Anne's parents let Larry understand that he was welcome in their home and maybe once a week they'd park in Sam Bechel's parlor and eat popcorn and watch TV or play games, or they'd be at Skip's house doing pretty much the same thing, or just talking.

They never went to Larry's house and never talked about it.

Larry had been showing them a brochure on the California Maritime Academy; he was pretty hepped up on the school and somehow it caught Anne's fancy so from between the two of them, Skip got little peace.

He ended up helping Larry nearly every evening with his math and English so that Larry could pass the examination; he was determined to pass it, and Anne kept urging Skip to help him. When she could she would come over and spend the evening with verbs transitive and compound sentences. It was, Skip thought, a conspiracy; he was finding out about the power of womanly persuasion.

And she wasn't the kind of a girl who talked him into anything and then left him stranded; she pitched in and she was a big help to both of them. Skip told himself that he really didn't want to be bothered with this because he wanted to wade through some engineering books, but Anne convinced him that he would be helping himself if he helped Larry.

So they began spending four evenings a week, seven to eleven, going through high school texts, and Skip was surprised to discover that he had missed a lot the first time around. He'd loafed along with a C average and now he wished that he'd studied harder.

Larry, who'd just skinned by, really had a job cut out for him, and in a way Skip expected him to chuck the whole thing, but Larry showed a stubbornness, a determination, that Skip had never seen before.

Anne kept applauding Larry's attitude; encouragement flowed out of her in a continuous stream. She talked their spirits up when they got low and Skip felt less like giving up.

One thing Skip was sure of; win or lose, Larry Wise had changed for good. He was constantly finding a surer grasp on himself and day-to-day living, and in spite of his hard work with the books, his work at the shop picked up and the other men gave him a genuine friendship.

He had earned it.

It was funny, Skip mused, how a fellow changed once he set a course and knew where he was going. He felt a bit amused at times because Anne always kept her eye on the compass, steering Larry, and at the same time guiding Skip, who was being towed along.

Anne made cocoa, tea, and coffee for them during their breaks; once in a while she brought cookies she had baked, and when Larry babbled on about the school she hung on to his every word as though she didn't want to do anything to dampen his enthusiasm.

Skip, who liked to be practical, kept pointing out the difficulties. "A thousand guys will take the exam, Larry, and the midshipman class is only one hundred. They'll take only the top grades."

"Skip, I've got to try," Larry said evenly. "I'm going to pass it. Isn't that right, Anne? Look, my old man goofed when he was my age. He had a chance to go to college and turned it down and went into the army. Only that didn't work out for him, and he discovered he'd blown it all just to get his father's goat. The point is, he didn't try, Skip. And I saw that I was doing exactly the same thing, goofing off, fighting it. All I had were the same stupid reasons he had and it's no good. Maybe I won't make it.

But if I don't, it won't be because I haven't given it everything I've got. That's what a guy has to do, Skip, give it everything. Failing is no disgrace. Not trying is. So let's go through that chapter on good paragraphs again, OK?"

After the Christmas holidays, Phil Osgood came back to work for Jim Vale, and Skip was called into the front office. Osgood was there, still flip and full of confidence and completely recovered from his accident. There were two other men there, well-known amateur sports car drivers, and Vale introduced Skip.

"This is Skip Hudson, who's been in charge of the cars and testing. Skinny McGuire from Santa Monica." They shook hands. McGuire was in his early twenties, a rail with thin shoulders and a suit that seemed too large for him. He had a firm grip and a rather thin smile, as though meeting mechanics was simply a bore to him and the sooner it was done with, the better. Then Vale turned to the other man. "This is Bill Shaw, from Monterey. He's been making a name for himself in Porsches." He waved Skip into a chair. "It's time to shape up a driving team; the LeMans race is held in the late spring and I want to give you men plenty of time in the cars. So we're going to spend some Sundays at Fawndale, then we'll enter the team in every sports car event right on up through May. OK?" He looked from man to man as though inviting them to comment, but Skip knew enough to keep his mouth shut. "I've already signed up three European *pilotos* to co-drive with you, but our concern now is to become familiar with the cars. So we'll see you at the course at ten o'clock, Sunday. OK?" He knew it would be and got up, shaking hands with each, but indicating that he wanted Skip to stay.

After the other three had gone, Vale lit a cigarette and leaned back in his chair. "I've gone over very carefully the work sheets you've turned in to Paul Lavery. Can Larry really change four wheels in eighteen seconds?"

"Consistently, if another man helps him pull the wheels."

"That's pretty good."

"It's better than good, Mr. Vale. It's the best you'll do."

"All right," Vale said. "It's the best then." He knocked ash off his cigarette. "This car you've been driving—do you think you've got everything wired down so it won't fall off?"

"Well, I've driven it at speed a total of a thousand laps and kept an accurate record of all the little details that needed attention. The engine hasn't been opened up and there have been no chassis repairs other than tires and brake pads. Of course, the engine's beginning to sound a little ratty and it's down on compression and the oil consumption has gone up somewhat, but it still gets around pretty well. Everything that's ever come loose has been wired tight and a modification sheet turned in to Lavery for the other three cars."

Vale tilted his big leather chair back and regarded Skip Hudson carefully. "You're a very thorough man, but let me ask you something: how many shifts have you missed out there? How many times have you over-revved that engine?"

"I haven't," Skip said honestly. "When I drive, Mr. Vale, I use a system. It's called: Watchwhattheheckyou'redoing."

Vale laughed. "I want you to drive Sunday. The others

will want to have a little go out there, and you might as well get in on it."

"If that's supposed to be a reward for something," Skip said, "then forget it. I've spent nearly every weekend at Fawndale, grinding around, shaking the bugs out of the cars, and it's no treat for me."

"And you've been paid for it," Vale said. "Drive Sunday."

"OK, I'll drive," Skip said and left the office.

That Saturday he went to the shop only long enough to get the cars loaded into the van, and to pack some tools and spare parts, just in case something broke. The day was cold and blustery although the sky was cloudless and the sun was bright.

In the afternoon he lounged around the house, did a few chores, then walked down town to his stepfather's body shop. Otto was trying to get a car out for a salesman who had made a late Friday miscalculation in traffic. The damage had been repaired and Otto had the car in the paint booth, baking the enamel on the fender. He was at his stand-up desk, making out the bill, when Skip leaned against the wall.

"What did Vale do, break down and give you the day off?" Otto asked.

"I think he realized how much overtime I was costing him," Skip said. "There's one thing about working hard; you're too busy to spend your money." He pulled a stool over and perched on it, his legs crossed. "It kind of looks like Jim Vale is going to let me go to France, Pop. I mean, he'll take Hermann, Luigi, and Larry, I'll bet. And I'm sure he'll make me the fourth man. I've met his drivers and they're going out tomorrow to run the cars around."

Otto finished the bill and put it aside. "Pretty well got your heart set on going to LeMans? I was there, many times, with the Mercedes cars. A lot of excitement. Something a man never forgets."

Skip frowned slightly. "It's a funny thing, but I've got the feeling that if I didn't go I wouldn't be absolutely sunk. You know, the people who think sports car racing is all glamour ought to work as a mechanic for awhile. After the race there's usually an engine to tear down, or a transmission to look into, or something."

"It's like a play, Skip. The audience sees the performance and rarely thinks about the rehearsal and the disappointments that took place behind that curtain, months before it opened." He picked up his pipe and tobacco pouch. "Let's go home."

Sunday was a bright day; the wind had died completely and it was warm in the sun. The four Lotus cars were parked side by side in the pits, three new ones and the slightly dingy work-horse that Skip had been driving. Of the four he liked the work-horse best. In a way he felt it more worthy to sit there in the racing pits than the other three, for it had suffered all the minor troubles so that the other three cars could be changed and modified without even leaving the garage. Skip felt that his car was like something that had undergone countless experiments so that the others could survive.

Jim Vale arrived in his sedan; he had the three drivers with him and they got out and looked over the cars. Climbing in them, they tried everything, started them up, and sat there, gassing the throttle.

Finally they got out of the cars and came over to where Vale stood.

He said, "Take the cars out for about twenty laps. Try not to break or bend 'em."

Skip said, "If you want, I'll show you the way around a few times."

Skinny McGuire reared back slightly. "Are you kiddin', sonny?" He laughed and walked over to his car and got in. Bill Shaw shrugged and looked at Phil Osgood; Skip pushed between them and went to the work-horse and started it up. It was beginning to sound rough and smoked faintly; he waited until the water temperature was at normal and the oil temperature started up, then accelerated out onto the course.

In his rear view mirror he saw McGuire and the others pull out and he kept his revs down, letting them pass him before they reached the sweeping banked turn. Skip fell behind and stayed there, letting them pick their way around a few times, building up their speed as they learned the course.

On the fifth lap they were beginning to turn up the wick going down the straight and McGuire was getting bolder in the first fast turn. Osgood and Shaw bunched up behind him, with Osgood trying to pass, but McGuire held him off.

Skip felt that he had trailed long enough and drifted through the fast turn, using top revolutions in third gear. This closed him up with the gaggle of cars braking down for the tight left hander. He passed Shaw on the outside, going deeper into the corner, then downshifted and cut across between Osgood and McGuire, and accelerated out of the turn in second place.

The Climax engine was down a bit on power; McGuire started to ease away along the short straight and Skip saw Osgood pulling up from behind. They ran alongside each other, with a sweeping right hand bend and the S's coming up. Osgood shot ahead when Skip braked early to enter the turn, and Osgood was ahead when they reached the curves, but his slide had carried him too far out for a fast line through the S's and by the time he got this straightened out, Skip had shot past, already accelerating hard in pursuit of Skinny McGuire.

Phil Osgood never gained back those seconds lost, for Skip Hudson was after Skinny McGuire with a vengeance. They came out of the tight hairpin at the end of the long straight together and Skip slip-streamed McGuire's faster car down the straight, but when they entered the first turn, instead of staying high on the outside as McGuire did, Skip cut low, cocked the Lotus into a drift and passed McGuire on the inside.

Jim Vale, who was keeping stop watches on everyone, laughed when the cars came around again and Skip Hudson had a three second lead over McGuire.

At the fifteenth lap, Skip had stretched the lead to eleven seconds, and from the sound of his exhaust down the straight, he was stroking it, backing off a little to save the engine. The Lotus was smoking steadily because of worn rings and tired pistons, but Skip kept lengthening his lead by a steady second a lap, and when Vale held up the blackboard with the number nineteen written on it, Skip waved and came in the next time around.

He had enough of a lead over McGuire to shut off the engine and open the door before McGuire came out of the hairpin turn. All the drivers pulled in and McGuire came over, his face set with anger.

"Sonny, the next time I get you on a course and you try to pass me, I'll nerf you good."

"Shut up," Jim Vale said matter-of-factly. "Skinny, you won't get close enough to bump him." He looked from one to the other. "Let me tell you what happened here. Skip, driving the work-horse, ran off and hid from you. Do you know why? Because he's driven that same car every weekend and piled up a thousand laps right here. Familiarity, that's the answer. Drive the car until you're wearing it. Drive the course until you can go fast in any kind of conditions. And that's what you're going to do if you're going to drive for me. Every Sunday you're going to be out here, driving the same car, going faster, until the old lap record is going to look like it was made by a motor scooter. Clear?"

They nodded and Vale turned away.

Skinny McGuire blew out a long breath and said, "I heard he was tough to work for, but not like this." Then he looked at Skip and grinned. "You really hit a nerve out there, kid. I always figured I could go fast in anything." He shook his head. "But after you dusted me in the first turn, all I saw was smoke."

Bill Shaw laughed. "Well, Skinny, he did offer to show you the way around, didn't he?"

"Maybe next time I'll listen," McGuire admitted and went over to talk to Jim Vale.

Chapter 10

HEADED FOR LEMANS

THERE was really no firmed up intention of taking the examination in Skip's mind: he had thought about it quite a bit but said nothing because of Larry.

He just didn't want Larry to think that he was riding along for the fun of it. Anne Bechel changed that; she could be a stubborn girl when she wanted to and Skip had to admit that she pushed him hard. And he really didn't mind, even when she said, "Skip Hudson, if you don't take that examination with Larry, I'll never speak to you again!"

So he checked with Paul Lavery and got the day off for both of them; he asked a good ten days in advance because he knew Lavery would have to schedule work around this absence; two men out of the shop would leave a gap in the work program. Skip explained to Lavery just what they were going to do and Lavery thought it was a good idea; he was the kind of a man who believed that you had to constantly better yourself.

That night, while they had dinner, Skip mentioned it to his mother and Otto, and they both looked at him a moment. Then his mother said, "Be sure and wear a suit. First impressions mean a lot."

"Heck, it's just a test."

"You heard me," she said, and he shrugged and went on eating.

Then he said, "Otto, do you think Larry's reputation will have any effect on his application?"

"Well, he's never been in Juvenile Hall, has he?"

"No. Close, but not in."

"Well, I don't think his traffic violations will be held against him. A lot of solid citizens pick up tickets."

"Larry collected them."

"I think they'll consider the irresponsibility of youth," Otto said. "Some good men have been in serious trouble in their younger days."

"You know, I sure hope he passes the examination," Skip said earnestly.

"What about yourself?" his mother said. "If you're going over there just to waste the state's time and money, I'd suggest that you stay home."

"I don't know, Larry's kind of got me excited. You know, I've been reading that brochure the Academy puts out. There's a lot there for the guy who buckles down and studies. A four year engineering education in three years, and a six week cruise every year. Not only that, you can get a commission in the navy when you graduate, or go into the merchant marine service as an engineer. It's a very highly rated school, Mom."

"I just can't imagine Larry in a uniform," she said.

Otto lit his pipe and spoke between puffs. "I have to admire Larry—for giving up a good—job for something like this. If I was a betting man, I'd put my money on him because now he wants something, and when a man wants something bad enough, he'll usually find a way to get it." He took his pipe out of his mouth. "His term will start in August and if he makes it, he'll have to give up the idea of going to LeMans with you and the cars."

"He knows that, Pop."

"I'll tell you what," Otto said, his manner excited. "If Larry passes the exam, I'd like to throw a party for him. Nothing real fancy you understand, but a few friends and Paul Lavery and his wife. I think he'd like that. What do you say?"

"It sounds like a great idea, Otto. I don't think Larry's ever had a party in his life."

"Everyone should have at least one," Otto declared. He puffed gently on his pipe. "Skip, does he ever talk about his mother?"

"She died ten years ago, before they moved here. Cancer, I think. He's mentioned her a few times but he doesn't like to talk about it."

"I shouldn't wonder," his mother said and got up to clear the table.

Otto wanted to work on his boat and Skip went out to help him; they didn't do much on it in the wintertime because the nights were too chilly, but now that it was decked and the cabin trunk finished, they could work inside with an electric heater.

At nine o'clock, Skip's mother came out and told Otto that one of his programs was coming on, so he put away his tools, unplugged the heater and they went inside. Skip got a piece of pie and kicked off his shoes before

curling up in the easy chair. During the commercials
he made two more trips to the kitchen, once for a glass
of milk, and the other for cookies to keep up his strength.

Skip hadn't worked on a customer's car for over a
month, since there was so much to do in preparation for
the LeMans race. Four new Coventry-Climax engines
arrived in crates and they had to be disassembled and
modified by a great deal of machine work, this filled his
days until it seemed that he lived inside the cyclone fence.

To the strategy of the race Jim Vale applied the thorough business approach, and after a long study he
reached certain conclusions. The course was long, with
one straightaway of four miles, where competing cars
reached 176 miles an hour and some had been clocked
at even faster speeds.

All the cars would be geared high and never run at
the full allowable revolutions, because in twenty-four
hours of racing a driver had to save his car as much as
possible.

Tests and experience with the engines had convinced
Vale that the power plant in the Lotus Elite coupe would
run great distances at sixty-eight hundred revolutions, yet
deliver power reliably. Gear ratios and transmission gears
were all carefully chosen to speed the car along while
running the engine within a narrow band of revolutions.

All modifications were made to produce the best power
between fifty-five hundred and sixty-eight hundred rpm,
and dynamometer tests on the engines modified by Skip
and Hermann showed a large output of power in that
range.

Jim Vale was aware that the Lotus factory team cars would not be out there puttering around; their cars were always outstandingly fast and reliable and their drivers the very best. But he was counting on being able to stay with them, and to last the distance while they ran out ahead and risked mechanical failure.

Carpenters came into the building and worked in one of the vacant storerooms for a week. Finally Vale called a meeting with Skip and the three drivers, produced a key, and took them into the storeroom and switched on the light.

On a long center table, built to scale, was the exact Sarthe circuit at LeMans. Model cars, to scale, sat on the course. Taking a pointer, Vale said, "On Monday and Wednesday nights, we'll meet here at eight." He pointed to a movie screen on the far wall and a projector. "I have films of the course, every corner, under all conditions. Gentlemen, we'll study this circuit until we know every bump in the road. OK?"

Shaw said, "That's a long drive from Monterey, Jim."

"So it's a long drive."

"And I've got a wife and two kids," Shaw said.

"Again, so?"

"So it's a lot of bother, Jim."

"I want things done right," Vale said.

"Sure you do, but it's overdoing it a bit, that's all."

"You can't make the big effort?" Vale asked. Then he let his brows bunch warningly. "All right, Bill, see the bookkeeper and have her give you a check."

"What do you mean? You're firing me?"

"Why not? Hudson can drive rings around you anyway."

Color came into Shaw's face, but he kept his voice even, although there was an edge to it. "You're a blunt man, Jim; I knew that before I agreed to work for you. But I never thought you could be a fool." He glanced apologetically at Skip. "Good luck, boy. You'll need it." Then he turned and walked out, slamming the door.

An uneasy silence filled the room; everyone's manner was strained and no one knew quite what to say. Jim Vale was not bothered. "Anyone else that can't make it on Monday and Wednesday evenings? I didn't think there was." He walked around to the other side of the table so that he faced them. "In this locked room we will work out a race strategy like Neubauer did with the Mercedes team cars, and we will stick with it. We will decide, on the basis of your driving ability in the months to come, who will charge out to break down the opposition and who will hang back to pick up the money when the opposition drops its cookies. OK?"

Skinny McGuire said, "Everything you say is OK, Mr. Vale. Don't you know that?"

Vale stared, trying to detect sarcasm, but McGuire's expression showed him nothing at all and Vale let it go. "Skip, I'll get you an FIA license; you leave the details to me. Now let's watch some movies."

He went back to the projector and turned it on. The others looked at each other and shrugged, then sat down while Vale killed the lights.

On Monday, Skip picked Larry up at his house; it was raining again and they drove thirty miles to Vallejo, asked at a filling station for directions, and drove to the Maritime Academy grounds, following a tree-lined road into a sheltered cove on the straits. The training ship was at the dock, and the buildings were all brick, large and impressive, surrounded by neatly trimmed lawns.

The examination was given in the mess deck, and the applicants were told that it was to be given in sections. A time limit governed each section and there was to be no smoking or talking.

Within thirty days, those who had passed the examination with a score of ninety or higher would be notified and sent additional papers to fill out. Those passing with a lesser score would be placed on a reserve list, to be called up if the academy could not fill their class with the A scores. Those failing would also be notified.

Then examinations began and only the rustling of paper and the push of pencils could be heard from the nearly three hundred young men crowded into the hall. Skip wasn't sure how he did on the first segment; he thought he had done well, but he couldn't be sure, for much of the examination was based on reasoning and logic. A man could fool himself on things like that.

It was four o'clock when they got out and as they climbed into the car, Larry said, "My mind's a complete blank. How do you think you did?"

"Well, I'm sure I passed it, but with what kind of a grade I wouldn't care to guess."

On the way home, Larry kept thinking of some of the questions and checking his answers with Skip, and when they were through, they still didn't know. Larry seemed almost afraid to hope.

Three Sundays of racing began to establish the drivers as to superiority. Skinny McGuire, after getting time in the car, demonstrated that three years of experience couldn't be discounted. He was generally a bit faster than Skip, but rougher on the car and more prone to get into trouble.

Even Phil Osgood occasionally showed the back of his car to Skip, but he couldn't do it regularly.

Skip's strong driving point was his smoothness; he went along steadily, surely, lapping the same each time, and in the long run this kind of driving always paid off. While Osgood was a sprint driver, and could show great speed, he couldn't do it lap after lap and traffic always slowed him a little.

The continual testing of the cars, alone, unbothered by anyone, had developed in Skip an unhurried style that was very impressive to watch, a style that made him a potentially great driver who did not break up the cars to go fast.

The rains continued; it was the season for them, and driving often became a miserable business, but it was something they had to master, going very fast over the wet track. In this department, Skip was clearly the fastest; he could out distance both Osgood and McGuire when the course was slippery, and Jim Vale was glad to see this, for many a LeMans race had been driven in a downpour. The French weather in the spring was fickle.

In Jim Vale's mind, McGuire was the superior driver

on a dry course, with Skip a close second and Osgood last. In the wet, Skip was faster and this condition, the weather, would determine who would be team leader once they got to France.

Vale had signed on a Belgian ace, a two-time LeMans winner, to co-drive the number one car, and like all team managers, the hope of winning was always placed on that set of drivers and car. If any car had to drop out of a team, it would never be the one in which the top driver circulated. Another car would be pulled in and handed over because to win you put the best men in the best cars.

Twenty-four hours, day and night; that was a real grind, and Jim Vale was glad he didn't have to do it. This feeling, however, did not prevent him from paying someone else to do it.

He stood by the pit wall, with binoculars in hand and his stop watch and clipboard handy, clocking them, watching them, checking them, catching every mistake they made out there.

In the last three weeks, Phil Osgood had spun his car four times. This worried Vale, for it meant that the driver was bobbling on the corners, over extending himself or the car when he should have had it firmly under control.

Vale toyed with the idea of replacing Osgood if this bad habit continued. He'd certainly say something to him when he came in.

Skip was the one Vale watched most closely; the boy was a natural, so very smooth, like Moss before the accident, and rather like Jimmy Clark, the present World Champion Driver.

Some men had that kind of talent, that control, that

ease, and some became great musicians, painters, or football heroes, and others became racing drivers.

He'd have to encourage Hudson, help him along; this was Vale's thought and now, watching him go on the track, he was sorry that he hadn't been around to watch this skill develop. The kid had been out there all alone, learning the hard way, trial and error.

A man really shouldn't miss a thing like that, Vale thought, and felt a selfish warmth for the boy.

Chapter 11

LARRY SUCCEEDS AT LAST

Being one of Jim Vale's fair-headed boys changed Skip's situation considerably, and he began to wonder about it. Vale, never shy where publicity was concerned, interrupted Skip's work almost daily, for Vale had some sports car magazine people as his guests and they were going to do a picture-story layout on the cars and drivers.

It seemed to Skip that he spent no effective time in the shop because he had to accompany Vale to restaurants, to San Francisco, and some evenings to Vale's luxurious home in the San Andreas hills where Vale entertained members of the press.

What bothered Skip most was the way Jim Vale talked; he understood that this was the "build-up," something for the newspapermen and magazine writers to hang a story on, but he didn't like to be referred to as a racing driver when he'd never won a race.

It seemed that Jim Vale wanted to do all the talking, even during the interviews with the drivers. Skinny Mc-Guire was not shy about relating the exciting story of

133

his life, and Phil Osgood enjoyed the attention and never missed a popping flashbulb, but Skip Hudson kept his mouth shut, hoping that the newspaper people would ignore him.

John Blazac was the editor of one of the leading sports car magazines, a rather small, gentle-mannered man who didn't push himself at all. At one of Vale's numerous parties, he got Skip aside and said, "He's got a great view from the terrace. Want to join me?"

"That sounds like a good idea," Skip said and went out with him.

The view was magnificent and the town in the valley below lay like multicolored jewels. They could see cars on the winding roads, headlights like bright fingers moving about on a dark cloth.

"Vale throws a nice party," Blazac said softly. He perched on the stone railing and put his hands on his knee. "How do you like working for him? I hear he's a real prima donna."

"I guess it's like any other job."

"Sure," Blazac said. "Say, is it true that your stepfather was one of the Mercedes-Benz racing mechanics before the war?"

"Yes."

"Would it be possible for me to meet him? Talk to him?"

"Sure. When do you want to do it?"

"Why, now if you think it's all right. We could cut out of here without being missed." He reached out and touched Skip on the arm. "Since Jim Vale likes to run everything I'd just as soon not tell him we're leaving."

He smiled and got off the railing. "My car's right down there."

They went down the inclining garden path and got into Blazac's car, a four-door Plymouth. As Blazac eased away, Skip said, "How come you tout sports cars and drive a Plymouth?"

Blazac laughed. "We've all got to be in some kind of a business, boy."

Skip gave him directions as they went along and then they pulled up out front and walked the path to the door. Skip went in first and Otto, reading, gave a start of surprise when the front door opened so suddenly. Then he saw Blazac and got up while Skip introduced them.

"Mrs. Hansen is at choir practice," Otto said. "Won't you sit down? I'll put on some coffee."

"I'll do that, Pop, because Mr. Blazac wants to talk to you." Skip walked into the kitchen and John Blazac sat down.

"You may not realize this, Mr. Hansen, but you're somewhat of a celebrity. There aren't many of the old Mercedes team around."

Otto Hansen smiled. "Let's have a clear understanding. I was a young man, not quite as old as Skip, and they let me change tires and wheels during the races. I never once put a wrench on any part of the engine or chassis. In fact, if I had so much as unfastened the hood, I would have been fired. So I wasn't a mechanic at all, just a part of the team. I'm like the surviving veteran of some past war, famous now because I outlasted other, better men."

"That certainly is modest of you," Blazac said, "but

you were there. You saw the glorious days." He took a small wire recorder and microphone from his coat pocket. "If you'd just talk to me about it, Mr. Hansen, I think we could get an article that would be of interest to our readers."

"Sort of making the silk purse out of the sow's ear?" He laughed and then Skip came in with a TV tray and the coffee maker. "Is Mr. Vale's party over?"

"Still going strong. Mr. Blazac wanted to talk to you."

"Yes," Otto said. He took his cup, added cream and sugar and stirred. "Mr. Blazac, let me ask you a straight question in the hope that I'll get a straight answer. Other than copy for your magazine, just what does all this promotional effort of Jim Vale's mean to you?"

"Nothing," Blazac said. "He's got some fast cars, he's going to Europe, and my magazine is interested in that. If he wins anything we'll write about it. If he loses, we'll write about that too, but only briefly. It's copy, Mr. Hansen. Nothing more, nothing less." He glanced at Skip. "Vale parades his three young hero-drivers around and that's all right; if they win anything we'll take their picture out of the files and print it. If they lose—" He shrugged and drank his coffee. "You see, I'm interested in everything and, yet I'm really not interested in anything except what has already happened." His glance went to Skip again. "But with you it's what's going to happen that matters, isn't it? Do you want to be a racing driver?"

"I like to drive," Skip said. "I think I do a good job of it. Not the best by any means, but good."

"The good don't get far in the racing business," Blazac

said. He looked at Otto. "How do you feel about him be-coming an International racing star?"

"Honest answer?" Otto asked. "I'd rather see him bag groceries in the Safeway store. But he has a life that he has to learn to live. I feel, and his mother feels, that he has to live it, make his own decisions. It's not easy for any man to face the fact that he may be ordinary, be-cause we all like to think of ourselves as something—well, better than that."

"It's kind of hard to say what I really want," Skip put in. "I keep thinking that it should be better than I have. By that, I mean I just can't see working forever for Jim Vale, although he pays good money." He shook his head. "And to tell you the truth, I can't see running around Europe as a race driver either. There's no sense in fooling yourself; you've got to keep going faster all the time and sooner or later you end up wrapped into a ball." He reached out and poured some more coffee. "This has been nagging me for some time now and I'm just begin-ning to make sense of it. You see, I want to be like Otto. Oh, not a body and fender man, but someone with some dignity. You're got to work with dignity, and Im not doing it. Not at all. When Larry got in trouble, I tried to help him, but I guess it was pretty selfish because I really wanted to help myself."

"Who's Larry?" Blazac asked.

"A boy that was headed for trouble," Otto said. "Jim Vale beginning to get under your skin, Skip?"

"No, it's not that. Any boss can get cranky once in awhile. It's sure hard to explain, Pop, but I want to do real things, things that mean something. I just haven't found anything at Vale's that I could dedicate myself to. You know what I mean? Like Mr. Freitas, the chemistry teacher; he could be making real money in some plant, but he wants to teach. He's dedicated to it. I think he'd go on teaching if they cut his salary." He shook his head again and fell silent.

John Blazac flicked his lighter and spoke from behind a cloud of cigarette smoke. "If I didn't like a job, I'd quit."

"That isn't what I meant to say," Skip said. Vale's is a good place to work. I guess it's the best. But where does it go?"

Blazac's eyes pulled down into narrow slits. "What does it matter?"

"I don't want to have to back-track three or four years of my life."

The phone rang and Otto said, "I'll bet that's Larry; he's called four times this evening."

Skip got up and went to the kitchen extension. "Hello. Oh, hi, Larry. I've been over at Vale's place. What's up?" He listened a moment, then put his hand over the mouthpiece. "Hey, Pop, did I get any mail today?"

"I don't know," Otto said, rising. "I came home late and didn't bother to look." He walked over to a small table in the hall and picked up some mail there. Then he came into the kitchen with a letter, holding it up so that Skip could see the return address: California Maritime Academy.

Skip took his hand off the mouthpiece. "Larry, I got a letter. What does yours say?" He spoke to Otto. "He hasn't opened it yet. What's that, Larry? Sure, come on over." He hung up and smiled. "That Larry, got the letter this afternoon and he's scared to open it. He's been over at Anne's house since seven o'clock. She's going to bring him over."

"Why don't you go ahead and open yours?" Otto suggested.

Skip took the letter and slapped it against his palm. "I guess I'll wait until Larry gets here."

"Feeling a little chicken?"

Skip grinned. "Yeah, now that you mention it. Maybe we'll let Anne open both of 'em. After all, she helped Larry a lot."

"You too," Otto said. "Your grades weren't that hot."

They went back to the living room where John Blazac waited. "I have a newspaperman's curiosity, Skip—what's so important about the letter?"

Skip explained the whole thing to Blazac. "Larry studied really hard to pass the exam, Mr. Blazac. It means a lot to him."

"What about you?" Blazac asked.

"That Larry, he infected me, I guess. Always talking about duty and tradition. That Larry's a real nut. And Anne kept pushing. A guy doesn't have a chance."

Blazac and Otto were watching him carefully, then Otto said, "If it doesn't mean so much to you, then open it. What if you failed? You still have your job."

"Pop, I didn't say it didn't mean much," Skip said defensively.

"How important is it then?" Blazac asked softly.

Faced with it, Skip knew. He said, "Important enough to make my hand shake." He held up the letter and it trembled a little. "I'm going to wait until Larry and Anne get here. We went into this together and we'll take the plunge together."

"Friendship is a wonderful thing," Blazac said. "Suppose you both passed?"

"What do you think bugs me?" Skip asked. "I'm afraid I didn't."

There wasn't much talk after that; then Anne and Larry came in. They looked at Blazac and Skip introduced them. Then Larry said, "Can't we go someplace—"

"We'll open them here," Anne said and took the letters.

Larry grabbed her wrist. "Suppose it's a bust-out?"

She looked at him softly. "Larry, you tried hard. Gave it everything you had. That's the important thing, isn't it?"

He nodded and Skip said, "I don't want to bust out either, so go ahead and open them, Anne." He licked his lips. "I don't care which is first as long as it isn't me." He grinned but it didn't come off and he knew it.

Anne took the letters, then slid her fingernail under the flap and opened the letter. She read. "Dear Mr. Wise: You have been accepted as a Midshipman in—"

She stopped reading when Larry made a strangling noise and pressed both hands over his face. Then he whirled and went into the kitchen. When Skip turned to follow him, Anne said, "Let him alone now. Give him a moment; he needs it."

They waited and it was very quiet. Then Larry came back, composed now. "I passed," he said softly, wonder-ingly. "Did you hear that? I passed."

Anne opened the other letter. "Dear Mr. Hudson: You

have been selected as an alternate—" She looked at Skip. "Do you want me to go on?"

He shook his head and tried to keep his expression from being crestfallen. "I just didn't make a high enough score for immediate acceptance." He looked at Blazac and began explaining, as though he needed to do this. "They take all the A grades immediately. After the other exams are given all over the state, the highest grades of the alternates are accepted, if there is any room left. I won't know the answer to that one until May."

"You'll be in Europe then," Blazac said.

"I just don't understand it," Larry said. "You're smarter than I am, Skip. How come—"

"I'm not smarter," Skip said. "You were in there fighting, Larry. You were giving it everything you had. I just wasn't, that's all. And that's what the exam is really for, to weed out the guys who don't give everything they have."

"But you helped me study," Larry said. "It isn't fair! Without you and Anne I'd never have made it and that's a fact!"

John Blazac got up. "I think I'd better be going." He shook hands with each of them, and Larry last. "Congratulations. You've cut out a career for yourself. Going for the engineering? Good choice there." Then he glanced at Skip. "Good luck with your decision."

He waved his hand when Otto moved to see him out. The door closed and moment later they heard Blazac drive away. Otto sat in his chair with his pipe and looked at Larry. "Midshipman Larry Wise. That's got a good sound to it. It has dignity. And a man must have that."

"Why don't I make some sandwiches?" Anne said and went into the kitchen. Skip sat down and picked up his letter and read it through.

Then he said, "A man has no way of knowing how he placed. Be near an A, but how near? I don't suppose they'd tell me either. It wouldn't do any good, really. I'm somewhere on a list, and every exam they give will produce some A grades and they'll lop names off the bottom of the alternate list. Mine can go and I'd never know it until May." He wiped a hand across his face. "How does a guy make up his mind anyway?"

"I don't know," Otto said seriously, "but certainly you will have to decide."

Anne came back with a tray of sandwiches. "Come on," she said, "don't look so down in the dumps. It isn't all that bad." Then she touched his hand. "What's too bad is that you didn't find out until now how badly you wanted to—" Then she smiled and offered the tray to Larry and Otto. "There's ham on rye, cheese and ham on white."

Larry said, "You know, I feel kind of numb all over." Then his expression sobered. "Mr. Hansen, there isn't anything that can go wrong now, is there? I mean, they can't up and change their minds, can they?"

"No," Otto said. "They checked your application thoroughly. They won't change their minds. You're in, Larry. Big as life."

"It sure is something," Larry said. "It'll take some getting used to."

"I wish I knew what my chances were," Skip said.

"But you don't know," Anne pointed out. "What you

have to decide is whether or not an engineering career
is worth taking the chance on. If you take it and quit
Vale, and it doesn't come off, I wouldn't want to see you
kicking yourself for it. There's no way to wire this, Skip.
It's a tight scene."

"I was counting on us going in together," Larry said.

"You can do things for yourself," Anne said frankly.
"Haven't you just proved that?"

"What I've got to decide," Skip mused, "is whether
to take a sure thing now with Jim Vale or to give it up
and gamble on three years of tough study." He wiped a
hand across his mouth. "How do I know which is right,
Pop?"

"You want a guarantee?"

"I guess that's what I want."

Otto shook his head. "There just isn't any. But one
thing for sure is that you'll have to tell Jim Vale now if
you decide to take a chance on acceptance. You can't
tell the man at the last minute that you're stepping out
and let him find another mechanic and driver."

"That's the way he'd do it, Pop."

"It's not the way you were raised to do it!" Otto said
flatly.

Skip looked at the floor, then at Larry. "Help me,
Larry. I really need it."

"You—you really want it?" He looked at Otto Hansen.
"It wouldn't be right for me to say, would it? Because
it would be what I wanted and not really what he
wanted." His glance swung back to Skip Hudson. "You're
the only friend I ever had who didn't try to work me for
something and I'd like to say it, but I can't. Your pop's

right. *You've* got to decide. For me it's easy. Tomorrow I'll just tell Paul Lavery that I'm leaving in August."

"Jim Vale may get so mad he'll fire you," Skip said. "You know how he gets."

"If he does," Otto said, "come and see me and I'll put you to work until your class starts."

"What about me, Pop?"

"I can't use two, and Larry spoke first." He smiled. "I'm not making it any easier for you, am I?"

"You're not even trying," Skip said, but he didn't sound bitter about it, or even resentful.

Chapter 12

DECISION

A SLEEPLESS night kept Skip dozing in snatches, and dreaming all sorts of things, yet always waking with his problem right there in the front of his mind.

This was, he guessed, the first really important decision he had ever made in his life, a decision that would affect him for the rest of it.

As soon as it was dawn he remained awake, but stayed in bed; there was no sense in stirring about and waking Otto or his mother. When it came time to get up, he dressed, went into the kitchen, and put on the coffee. Soon his mother came in, gave him a hug and turned to the refrigerator.

"Otto told me about the letters you and Larry got. Larry must have been very proud of himself."

"Yes, he was," Skip said, sitting down at the dinette. "I don't think Larry will make any more trouble for anyone, or himself. I don't think he's ever going to be afraid again that people won't notice him." He fell silent for a moment. "Mom, there never was much difference between

Larry and me, except that you and Otto have always noticed me. You know what I mean? I always had the idea that I was appreciated, even when I didn't deserve it."

Otto came in, his slippers padding on the tile floor; he checked the progress of the coffee and sat down across from Skip. "Get much sleep?"

"Not much."

The coffee maker gave a final gurgle, announcing that it had completed its cycle and Skip's mother got out the cups and served them. Then she turned back to the stove.

"All night long I've been thinking hard, Pop. You know, a guy just can't make a decision like this on his feelings. It's got to come out of his head. It's got to be honest, even if it hurts a little."

"That's where it's got to come from, all right," Otto said. "I guess you've made up your mind then."

Skip nodded his head. "I've decided. You know, I like cars. I bought that Healey when I was fifteen after saving paper route money for three years, and it took a year to fix it up. Then I got that spare time job at the used-car lot." He paused to drink some coffee. "I guess I had it figured what I wanted to be, a mechanic."

"You're a good mechanic," Otto said. "A natural talent with tools, and a good ear for engine work."

"That's not what I'm getting at, Pop," Skip said. "When I went to work for Vale, I figured that this would be about it. That would be where I got a reputation, set myself up." He shook his head. "But the truth of it is, I could go on and on and still never know anything."

"What do you mean, not know anything?"

Skip frowned, trying to find the words. "I can tear down an engine, rebuild it, and even modify it after someone else has figured out how to do it exactly right. I can change a suspension system on a race car to handle like the driver wants, but I don't know why it's done. I can't really make anything, because I just don't know anything." He put his palm to his cheek and rocked his head from side to side. "Boy, when I think of the day I went to Vale's to ask for the job; I was sure I knew it all. I honestly felt that I was offering him the best deal of his life. You know, Pop, Larry and I were on opposite ends of the line; he felt that he couldn't do anything and I was sure I could do it all."

Otto tipped his head forward to hide his smile and to meet his coffee cup half way. "Admitting that is real progress," he said. "There have been times when your positive attitude has been irritating."

"That's why I'm going to tell Jim Vale that I won't be going to France with him," Skip said. "I'm going to the academy and I'm going to learn something. Maybe I'll go to sea and maybe I won't. I may even go into the Navy. I don't know what I'll do, but I'll tell you this, Pop, whatever I do, I'll know something. Do you understand what I mean?" He glanced at his watch. "My gosh! I've got to pick Larry up in three minutes! Good-by." He gave his mother a quick kiss and dashed out, slamming the door.

"A young man in a hurry," Otto said and took the plate of bacon and eggs she handed him. Then he took her hand and held it. "Proud of your boy, Ellen?" He patted her hand and then began to eat. "It would be nice to be invisible and stand in Jim Vale's office when he gets the real word from two young men who know it."

"Otto, do you think he'll fire them because of this?"

"What does it matter? Is he really important? Or his job? Jim Vale will be dealing with two men who know where they're going." Otto laughed. "He doesn't have a chance."